The Lovely Adventuress

"So you're an orphan cast upon the world," Quentin Travers observed. "And how do you intend to make your way in the world?"

Humor not quite masking the determination in her violet eyes, Vanessa said airily, "Oh, I shall find myself a wealthy merchant, the richer the better! Mama was the daughter of an earl, you see, and that counts a great deal with persons who are desirous of entering society."

"There are other things in life besides money," he said softly.

"Not when you've been all your life without it! And I shall give good value to my merchant. I shall advertise my aristocratic connections and be a decorative addition to his drawing room. And in return I shall have a carriage and pair and velvet curtains in all the salons!"

Quentin Travers was charmed. Here was a young woman as extravagantly honest as she was beautiful. But would she be so frank if she realized she was talking to one of England's most sought-after bachelors? Quentin's mouth twisted with a cynical smile. He thought not. . . .

Peggy

Vanessa

Catherine Fellows

A DELL BOOK

Published by
Dell Publishing Co., Inc.
1 Dag Hammarskjold Plaza
New York, New York 10017

Dell ® TM 681510, Dell Publishing Co., Inc.

ISBN: 0-440-17181-4

Printed in the United States of America

First printing—January 1978

Chapter One

The matched bays took the difficult turn through the lodge gates of the Court without slackening their stride, but the lodgekeeper, hurrying out for a view of the departing curricle, had no doubt that it was Mr. Travers. Two days after he was expected, as well, as his stepmother would doubtless tell him in no uncertain terms at the first opportunity.

Mr. Travers, meanwhile, in happy ignorance of the nature of his reception, slowed his horses to a gentle trot to admire the golden sheen cast by the evening sun on the ornamental lake and neighboring woodlands. It was a pleasant vista and he let his eyes dwell on it appreciatively, smiling slightly as his groom remarked prosaically that the June weather was burning the grass off.

"You have no soul, Walker," he said.

"That's as may be, but I'll wager there's no grazing left for the hunters on the top fields!"

"Then move them to the lower paddock," Mr. Trav-

ers recommended, halting the bays before the impos-
ing portico columns of the Court. Passing the reins to
the groom, he stretched his stiff shoulders as he
climbed down from the curricle and mounted the
wide steps. As he commenced the second flight, his
butler, alerted by the hoofbeats on the gravel, drew
open the double doors with infinite dignity and
bowed his master into the hall.

Responding to his greeting, Mr. Travers said, "Are
the ladies well, Hobson?"

Hastening to take his hat and driving gloves, Hobson replied that he believed they were both in good
health, and indicated the assortment of correspon-
dence on the silver tray. Going through it idly, Mr.
Travers said, "I expect they have dined, so you may
tell the chef to send me up something cold to the
breakfast parlor. I stopped to eat on the road, so I
want none of his usual elaborate two courses!"

Anxiety chased quickly across Hobson's face. Receiving no reply, Mr. Travers looked up inquiringly,
and in some confusion the butler coughed. "It so happens that dinner has been put back tonight, sir. Miss
Caroline returned late from an excursion and it is due
to be served in half an hour."

"In that case I will join Mrs. Travers and Miss Caroline when I have washed. I daresay they will excuse
my not changing on this occasion."

Still sorting through the collection of bills and gilt-
edged invitations, he did not see the expression of
pure agony in Hobson's eyes as they rested on his apparel, though indeed there was nothing a clothes
brush and duster would not swiftly set to rights. Agony gave way to indecision and indecision to resolve.
In a voice that trembled only slightly, he said, "I be-

lieve Mrs. Travers wished to see you most urgently, sir!" and retreated at a speed entirely at variance with his rigid training and years of service.

Mr. Travers watched him go in mild surprise. Left to wonder whether the urgency was such that he should postpone his wash, he decided to seek enlightenment of his half sister and, ascending the stairs to the second landing, tapped on her door. Entering at her invitation, he beheld her seated at her dressing table, but as their eyes met in the mirror she leaped to her feet, scattering brushes and ribbons and ornaments as she turned.

"*Quentin!*"

"My appearance seems to evoke a most unflattering response," he observed mildly. "Why '*Quentin*'?"

Her gray eyes beginning to dance, she said, "Then you haven't seen Mama!"

"I have just been informed by Hobson, in what I can only describe as a very odd manner, that she wished to see me!"

Caroline chuckled. "The poor man was forbidden by Mama to tell you, but he couldn't let you go to your fate without a warning!"

A suspicion of events began to take hold in Mr. Travers's mind, and observing his expression, Caroline nodded in confirmation. "You are perfectly right! She has invited Another One!"

Mr. Travers let out his breath in exasperation. "Who is it this time?"

"Elizabeth Gnosill—I should say *Lady* Elizabeth Gnosill! She and Lady Wrenshaw have been here since Tuesday and Mama is fit to burst her stays because she thought you were coming two days ago!

Quentin, you won't let Mama make you offer for her, will you?"

"No, dear sister, I will not!" Mr. Travers returned, a trifle grimly.

"Good!" She gave him a sunny smile. "Actually it has been rather entertaining. Mama, of course, didn't *say* why she'd invited them—one doesn't—but all of us *knew*, and these last two days Lady Wrenshaw has been wondering aloud when they were going to see you, and poor Mama keeps repeating that she cannot think what has occurred to delay you. And Elizabeth is furious but daren't show it!" Her lively face changing from amusement to disapproval, she said, "Lady Wrenshaw is forever pointing out to Mama how virtuous and accomplished she is, and I suppose one must admit that she is very handsome, even though she must be at least five and twenty, but I don't think she is at all amiable, and I shouldn't care to have her for a sister-in-law!"

"Don't perturb yourself—she won't be!" He lowered himself into an adjacent easy chair, dwelling with irritation on his stepmother's latest matchmaking attempt. In general he held her in both respect and affection; he had no memory of his own mother, who had died in his infancy, and from the moment of her marriage to his father his stepmother had treated him as though he had been her own son. It was only in her determination to choose him a suitable wife that they could not agree. Mr. Travers admitted that her reasons for wishing him bound in wedlock were praiseworthy—the estates were entailed and if he were to die without an heir they would accrue to his ever-hopeful cousin Herbert. He had taken a violent dislike to cousin Herbert on their first meeting and he had no more desire than his stepmother to think that he might one day be treading the marble floors of the Court, but neither could he accept the vision of a future with any of the damsels she had been ruthlessly thrusting at him for the past few years.

For this his earlier experiences were to blame, when as a callow and somewhat tongue-tied young man he had discovered that even the haughtiest of the season's debutantes would warm to him amazingly the minute they found he was the owner of a large country seat, two smaller estates, a hunting lodge, and a rather fine town house in Mayfair. Not one of the young ladies so far lured to the Court could be acquit of an interest in these, and he had more than once thought of starting the rumor that he was in financial difficulties.

He roused himself to find Caroline watching him with an air of expectancy, but she merely pointed out that if he was joining them for dinner he had best go and change.

Mr. Travers's inner self was subjected to a severe and prolonged struggle. Finally, well aware that he was giving way to an ignoble impulse, he said, "But I'm not!"

She stared at him, round-eyed. "What will you tell Mama?"

Apologetically, he said, "I'm afraid I'm not going to tell her anything. Craven it may be, but I'm going to make a run for it!"

"But . . ." She broke off as they both heard Mrs. Travers's unmistakable tread on the landing outside, and without a second's hesitation she propelled him into her dressing room. He did not have time to close the door and, in his haste, cannoned into a tall cheval glass so that it swung backward and forward with an ominous creak that under normal circumstances would certainly have drawn his stepmother's attention. Fortunately, at that precise moment she was too much taken up with her own troubles to notice.

Bursting in, she exclaimed forcibly, "Where *can* the provoking creature be? I've a letter here from Clara Millington and she says he left her place on Monday and declared he was coming home!" She sank into the chair recently vacated by Mr. Travers, so that Caroline found she was watching her in fascination, mortally afraid that the warmth of the previous occupant might communicate itself to her. Mrs. Travers, however, was fanning herself with the folded pages of her letter as though trying to blow away her agitation.

"He must have gone on somewhere else without telling me, and how I can summon the courage to face Lady Wrenshaw across the table again tonight I do not know!"

Casting a nervous glance in the direction of her dressing room, where the looking glass still swung gently to and fro, Caroline said, "Could you not say you have just been informed he is unwell, or has met with a slight accident, or something of that nature?"

"If you don't know your brother by now you ought to!" Mrs. Travers returned tartly. "I should no sooner have got the words out of my mouth than he would walk in large as life to expose it all for the lie it was!"

Acutely aware of Mr. Travers only yards away, Caroline fought back a desperate desire to giggle. "Yes . . . well I do not know what to suggest."

"No more do I! If he hasn't arrived by tomorrow I shall take to my bed with palpitations, which I dare swear will be true enough by then! Lady Wrenshaw, from common civility will be forced to leave, though I don't suppose for a moment she will believe it, and I shall never be able to face her again as long as I live! And Elizabeth such a charming girl in every way! Where *can* he be?"

Stoutly, Caroline said, "*I* don't find Elizabeth charming, Mama, and I must tell you that I don't think Quentin would either!"

"No! Left to himself he would choose someone completely ineligible," Mrs. Travers replied unguardedly. "If you knew . . ." She closed her lips, realizing the unsuitability of the disclosure, and got up from the chair, as near distraction as was possible in one of her normally capable temperament. "I suppose I must go down, though I shan't be able to swallow a mouthful!"

She trailed out, shaking her head, her state of mind such that she had not noticed her daughter was nowhere near prepared to follow her, and Caroline collapsed on her stool, torn between laughter and genuine pity for her mother's predicament.

As Mr. Travers reentered, she said reproachfully, "Poor Mama! How can you, Quentin?"

"It is reprehensible, I know," he admitted. "But consider the alternatives! If I go down and display only ordinary courtesy they will have it settled between them that the wedding day is as good as fixed, and if I let them see that I have absolutely no interest in the girl, she and Lady Wrenshaw will be affronted and your mama will be as much embarrassed as she is by my nonappearance. Quite apart from the fact," he added feelingly, "that I shouldn't hear the last of it for a twelvemonth!"

"You wouldn't, of course," Caroline agreed. "And Elizabeth is *not* charming, in spite of what Mama says. She had been here three whole days before she graciously informed me that I need not continue to address her as *Lady* Elizabeth!" She grimaced, then, in a more practical spirit, said, "The gong will be going in less than ten minutes."

"I'll slip out by the side door while you're all at dinner. Be a good girl and go down and tell Hobson that if he breathes a word of my coming here I'll retire him without a pension!"

Hastily trying to smooth her tumbled brown locks, Caroline gurgled with laughter. "Poor man! But what of Mama? I know it is entirely her own fault, but she means it for the best and it would be unkind to leave things as they stand!"

He rubbed her cheek with his finger. "I know. I'll write a letter with some excuse or other and get the stagecoach driver to post it along his route. I can't travel far with the bays tonight and I don't want her to think I'm as near as fifty miles from the Court." He opened the door a crack as he spoke. "Where are Lady Wrenshaw's and Elizabeth's rooms situated?"

"In the other wing, but I expect they have gone down by now, anyway. I must rush if I'm to catch Hobson!" Snatching up her reticule and shawl, she turned at the door to give him a conspiratorial grin. "Good luck!"

He raised a hand in silent acknowledgment and settled himself for his short wait, and when the gong's reverberations had died away, made haste to absent himself before he could be caught by the housekeeper on her evening rounds.

In the stables, his command to have the bays set to again was received by Walker with astonishment and a demeanor that suggested that the order amounted to active cruelty.

"But they've barely been dried off, sir," he protested.

Mr. Travers replied that he was not proposing to take them to John o' Groats, and in ten minutes, having pledged the entire stable staff to secrecy on pain of instant dismissal without a reference, he was once more bowling along the gravel drive. He checked at the gates to lay a similar charge on the lodgekeeper, then turned the bays on to the open road, and what, though not usually fanciful, he found he regarded as freedom.

The exhilarating sense of release, however, shortly turned to remorse. The bays responded courageously when he eased off the reins, but their lowered heads betrayed their tiredness and he pulled them back to a walk. By the time he reached the village of Priors Cross he knew it would be inhuman to ask them to go farther, and accordingly turned under the archway into the stableyard of the Angel, a house which had been much patronized by him in his youth when he had first discovered the twin lures of strong ale and convivial company.

The ostler who came out to him was considerably surprised to be asked to stable the bays for the night when Mr. Travers's place, as he knew, was only six miles' distant; but when, after watching them rubbed down and fed, Mr. Travers went into the inn, the landlord accepted his request for a room without a blink. Mr. Travers, Roberts knew, was not normally given to odd quirks, and if he wished to put up at the inn instead of his own home, he doubtless had his reasons. He therefore allocated him his principal bedchamber and, noticing that he was apparently traveling without a valet, sent up a man to pull off his boots and shave him if he should require it.

In fact, Mr. Travers was so well pleased with his apartment and the attentions to his comfort that by the time he had washed and changed and partaken of an excellent meal, he was more than half decided to stay where he was for a few days. His fishing gear was still in the curricle, and the river, only two fields distant, afforded very satisfactory sport for a keen angler.

Thus it was that the following morning found him up at sunrise and clad in garments suitable for a protracted vigil on the river bank. Having collected a package of food from the kitchen and his rods from the coach house where they still reposed in the curricle, he set out across the yard, but paused halfway, his attention caught by the unprecedented circumstance of the Holyhead to London mailcoach having come to a halt before the inn doors. Since he knew the Angel was not contracted to supply horses for the Mail, Mr. Travers was mildly curious as to the cause of the unauthorized stop, particularly as it soon became apparent that there was a heated argument in progress between the coachman and a lady passenger. As he watched, Roberts appeared at his doorway, and an ostler, attracted by the commotion, moved inquisitively closer. Temporarily abandoning his fishing, Mr. Travers went over to join them.

The young lady, for from her back view she appeared to be young, was saying heatedly, "No doubt if I had informed you instead that she was suffering from the smallpox you would have flung both us and our baggage out by the roadside ten miles back! I tell you she cannot travel farther without danger to her life and if you would get our trunk down instead of abusing us it would be better for all! I am fully aware that you must keep to your time schedule, but this is the direst emergency!"

In reply, the coachman spread his bulk aggressively across the box seat and retorted that his chief responsibility was for the Mail. The guard joined in to complain that they had to clock in at Daventry and he would be fined if they were late, and the ostler, who had been casting a professional eye over the team, advised the young lady to move away from the wheeler or she was liable to be kicked. Here Mr. Travers, his gentlemanly instincts rising to the fore, decided to intervene.

Stepping forward, he said politely, "Can I be of assistance, ma'am?"

She swung around and he witnessed a face of startling beauty. Her violet eyes were narrowed with anxiety and a flush of anger heightened her complexion, but never had he seen more perfect features.

A flicker of thankfulness crossed her face and she took a hesitant step toward him. "If you would get my sister carried into the inn and persuade this odious man that we cannot possibly stay here without our luggage, I should be extremely grateful to you, sir."

Feeling in his pocket for suitable coins to alleviate the situation, Mr. Travers beckoned the ostler to assist with the trunk and climbed into the coach to bring out the unfortunate traveler. She was collapsed in the corner with the other two passengers attempting to support her, and as he bent to lift her he saw that her eyes were closed and her breathing labored and shallow. With sharpened concern he picked her up and backed out of the coach, saying to the landlord, "Quickly! Where can I put her?"

Roberts hesitated, disapproval written over his face. Clearly he did not relish taking in an unknown and extremely sick girl, but Mr. Travers said authoritatively, "Hurry, man!" His tone was impatient, and with a shrug the landlord led the way through the entrance hall and up the stairs to a bedchamber on the first floor.

Mr. Travers laid his burden gently on the fourposter bed in the room indicated, but her sister, following closely behind, exclaimed, "No, no! I beg your pardon, but she must not lie flat! Hold her up so that I may put the pillows behind her!"

Complying, Mr. Travers studied the sufferer's face. She was ashen pale and her chest heaved with the effort of drawing each breath. Inexperienced in the sickroom, he wondered if she was dying, and carefully keeping any excessive anxiety from his voice, said, "Shall I have a doctor summoned? She seems very ill."

She shook her head. "Not yet. I have her medicine and inhalent in the trunk. If they do not bring about an improvement, then we will send for one, but I doubt if he would be able to do any more for her than I can. I am used to dealing with her, and now she is out of the coach the situation is no longer desperate. It was the traveling." She laid her sister back against the pillows and moved purposefully to the door where Roberts was hovering. "If you please, I shall need a basin of very hot water immediately!"

His eyes strayed to the luggage, which was far from new. "Yes, Miss . . ."

"Hartland," she supplied coolly. "And I shall require accommodation for myself and my sister for at least two nights." As he still showed reluctance, she said, "I should like the hot water at once."

She turned away as though in no doubt of the order being obeyed and began to undo the cords binding the trunk. Mr. Travers, after directing a meaningful look at Roberts, went to the other side to assist her. In a low voice, he said, "Are you sure you would not rather I called a doctor?"

Shaking her head, she lifted the lid and extracted two bottles and measured a spoonful from one of them. Her sister grimaced as she swallowed it and managed a wan smile.

"Vanessa . . ." she whispered.

"Do not try to talk!"

Mr. Travers, receiving the hot water at the door, dwelt appreciatively on the name, heedless of his burning fingers. She took it from him with a brief smile of thanks and poured into it some of the mixture from the second bottle. A pungent aroma immediately filled the room, and carrying the bowl across to the bed, she stood for a moment, her face showing indecision for the first time.

"Helen, are you able to sit up?"

In response her sister struggled to support herself in an upright position, but plainly it taxed her strength to the limit, and Mr. Travers, susceptible to the appeal in the violet eyes, moved over to hold her up.

He was rewarded by a warm glance. "Thank you. The water has to be hot and I am so afraid of spilling it on her. She has enough to contend with already." Her eyes strayed around the room. "Do you think you could pass me that towel from by the washbowl?"

With a fleeting thought for his intended fishing, Mr. Travers obliged. Almost as though she had read his mind, she said quickly, "I should not be asking you to do all this! You have been more than kind and I must not take further advantage! If you would ask the landlord to send in a chambermaid I need not trespass any further upon your time!"

Mr. Travers knew that unless he endorsed the order she would not find Roberts overready to comply. Innkeepers were quick to sum people up, and here were no wealthy travelers to have their every whim indulged. If the Misses Hartland had stepped down from a private chaise with an abigail in attendance, they would have been bowed into the second best bedchamber, which Mr. Travers knew was lying vacant at the rear of the inn.

He smiled down on her. "I was merely going fishing, so the time is not important. Do you wish me to drape the towel around her head?"

She flushed slightly and nodded, pleased to find him so quick to understand her requirements. "If you would be so good."

His own eyes watering from the vapor, Mr. Travers sat holding the towel and covertly studying the intent little face opposite him. Miss Vanessa Hartland he judged to be some nineteen years of age, and closer inspection did not cause him to revise his first impression of her beauty. Besides her remarkable eyes and classic features, she had a fine, flawless skin, framed by raven dark ringlets, which, now that she had discarded her bonnet, he could see were secured with a comb on the back of her head.

She looked up and caught him watching her but was in no way discomposed.

"Thank you," she said. "I think she will do now."

Helen was unveiled and emerged moist and red in

contrast to her previous pallor. Her eyelids were heavy and it was obvious that she still breathed with difficulty, but Mr. Travers was astonished by the improvement in her condition. She smiled on him and said faintly, "you have been most kind to two strangers, sir, and I do not know what we should have done without your assistance. We do not even know your name."

He bowed. "Quentin Travers at your service, ma'am, and may I say how happy I am to see you so much restored. Your sister would not have me summon help and it is plain to me now that you have a most excellent nurse, but I will tell you that if it had been left to me I should have sent for an army of doctors!"

"Another few miles and they would have been needed," Vanessa said, busying herself about the room. "Helen could not possibly have reached Daventry! If that wretched coachman had put us down when the attack came on all this might have been averted!"

Folding the towel neatly, she placed it back on the washstand and turned to hang her redingote in the wardrobe.

Noting that she was accustomed to performing these tasks herself, Mr. Travers said, "I should not make yourselves too much at home in here. You are fronting on to a busy postroad, and since your sister's disorder affects her breathing I think you would be better situated at the back of the inn away from the dust."

She made a wry face. "I daresay, but the landlord was within an ace of refusing to take us in and who can blame him? If I demand another bedchamber he

may decide to dispense with our custom altogether
and Helen could not travel another yard today!"

"Nevertheless, I would ask you not to unpack until I
have spoken to him." Accompanying his words with a
smile, he let himself out and went to inform Roberts
that there was now no danger that he might find himself with a corpse on his hands. The landlord's manner
indicated that recovered or not, chance travelers with
decrepit luggage were not, in his opinion, desirable
denizens of the Angel.

Mr. Travers smiled gently. "Oh, come, Roberts.
They are obviously gentlewomen and would not request the accommodation if they were unable to meet
your bill. And I will tell you that I find the younger
Miss Hartland of far greater interest than any sport
the river could offer me!"

"Aye," Roberts returned, his expression unchanging.
"I had your gear brought back in from the yard. I
didn't think you'd be going out again this morning."

Mr. Travers grinned. "Precisely! I also feel that Miss
Helen Hartland's health would benefit from a bedchamber at the rear of the inn. When you inform them
of their change of room, perhaps you would tell them
that if Miss Hartland is well enough, Mr. Travers
would esteem it an honor if they would join him for
breakfast at about ten o'clock."

"You were born to be hung," Roberts observed,
with a sudden, surprising lack of respect. "It had better be the private parlor, I suppose, otherwise you'll
have Mrs. Moorcroft and her companion with their el-
bows in your coffee cups, the better to listen. A nos-
ier pair I never met!"

Mr. Travers approved the private room and pursued
a leisurely course to his room to change into garments

more fitted to the entertainment of two ladies. Never at any time ostentatious in his dress, it was not his custom to draw attention to himself in the country by assuming town apparel, and the coat that he eased himself into, though perfectly cut, was modest in both color and style. His boots were of the finest but their surface brilliance had become a little dulled over the last few days while he had been traveling without his valet. Surveying himself critically, Mr. Travers decided his whole appearance lacked the polish of this individual's expert ministrations, and he looked more like a country squire. He raised a hand to straighten his shirt points, twitching at them in dissatisfaction, and, in doing so, caught sight in the mirror of the valuable signet ring he habitually wore. On an impulse he took it off and slid it into his pocket and, smiling in derision at himself, went downstairs.

After checking on the bays and perusing the morning papers, he hopefully awaited the Misses Hartland in the private parlor, and was rewarded some half hour later by their appearance. As he drew back their chairs from the table, he became aware that his previous contact with Helen had left him with an entirely false impression. He had seen her only in the grip of a distressing illness, but seeing her almost recovered now and with her hair becomingly arranged, he realized she was an extremely lovely young woman. Lacking her sister's perfect beauty, there was yet a softness in her features that made her if anything the more attractive of the two. As she smiled her thanks and moved forward to take the place he was offering, he also noted that she walked with a pronounced limp. She was not awkward—indeed, in some inexplicable fashion she still moved smoothly and held herself erect—but there was no possibility that it could pass unnoticed.

Mr. Travers felt it was a pity. Within seconds of their entering the room he had confirmed his belief that they were not in easy circumstances. Their high-waisted gowns were in the latest mode but made up in inexpensive muslins and trimmed only with rib-bons, and the shawls about their shoulders, though of costly silk, had the faintest tinge of yellow as though they had been laid away since more prosperous days. Impecunious young women of gentle birth must rely heavily on making good marriages. The younger Miss Hartland would doubtless experience no difficulty, but Helen's disability might prove a serious draw-back.

He settled her at the table and, turning to perform the same office for Vanessa, was surprised to see what was almost an expression of antagonism in her eyes. It was gone in a second, and wondering what he had done to deserve it, Mr. Travers signed to the waiter to begin serving.

For a girl of small stature and delicate appearance, it seemed Vanessa possessed a healthy appetite. View-ing her plate, Mr. Travers wondered if she had over-estimated her capacity, and catching her eye, he beheld, for the first time, a glimmer of amusement.

"I was a little apprehensive before the start of our journey yesterday and found myself quite unable to swallow anything," she explained. Her eyes narrowed in a sudden smile. "You won't betray us if I tell you we have never traveled before?"

"Certainly no one would guess it," Mr. Travers said truthfully. "Have you come far?"

"From Shifnall." He waited for her to expand, but

her attention had returned wholly to her plate. Pushing across a dish of ripe strawberries that he felt certain were bound to take her fancy, he turned instead to Helen. "Would you consider me impertinent if I addressed you as Miss Helen and Miss Vanessa?"

Even such a simple question caused her to flush and it was plain she was agonizingly shy, but she managed to make her voice composed. "Of course not, Mr. Travers. It can be very confusing to conduct a conversation with two Miss Hartlands."

"It would be if your sister were not so busy repairing the omissions of yesterday," Mr. Travers observed, a trifle acidly. "Tell me, Miss Helen, since I must be vulgarly blunt in order to satisfy my curiosity, what was your destination before the unfortunate interruption in your journey?"

"London, sir. We intended to stay a week or so, then continue on to Brighton."

"Shifnall to Brighton!" He raised his brows. "You are a brave woman to attempt such a distance!"

"My sister felt the sea air of Brighton would benefit my health," Helen said, betraying confusion.

"I should have thought there were nearer coastal resorts, similarly beneficial!"

"None that would serve my purpose so well," Vanessa retorted.

Her tone clearly discouraged further inquiry, and after regarding her for a moment, Mr. Travers said abruptly, "How old are you?"

She gave him a frigid glance. "I cannot see how it concerns you, Mr. Travers, but I have no objection to telling you. I am twenty-one!"

He caught a quick flash of surprise on Helen's face and said, "And untruthful! Forgive the question, it was ill bred I know, but it seemed to me that you are neither of you very old to be embarking on such an undertaking unprotected. Have you friends or relatives to go to in London?"

"No," she returned distantly. "It is my experience that people are frequently better off without either. I assure you, Mr. Travers, that we are quite capable of looking after ourselves."

Mr. Travers kindly refrained from pointing out the obvious error in this statement, but she colored slightly and, rising to her feet, said, "Will you excuse me for a moment? I recall that I have left my handkerchief in my room."

She left the parlor, and Mr. Travers turned to Helen with a quick disarming smile. "She is perfectly right. It is no concern of mine."

Distressed, she said, "Oh, no, Mr. Travers! We are both very sensible of how much we owe you. We should have been in a sad case without your help this morning." She hesitated. "I beg you will not take offense at what Vanessa said. We have had many troubles recently and she has taken the responsibility for so many difficult things. . . ." She gave a faint, self-deprecatory smile. "I fear that I am not the help to her that I should be. I lack the courage for important decisions, and she has had to . . ." She broke off as Vanessa returned and threw her a pleading look. "I was just telling Mr. Travers how grateful we are for everything. The situation of our new bedchamber is a vast improvement. We have a most delightful view over the orchard."

Vanessa dimpled suddenly. "Indeed, yes. I beg your pardon, and I will confess that my sister's manners are a good deal better than mine!" She looked at him curiously. "What means did you employ on the landlord?"

"None were necessary," he replied blandly. "I did no more than inform him that my interest in the trout had waned."

Vanessa swept him a curtsey. "Delightfully phrased. And how comforting to know you possess such influence!"

"Oh, it is merely that I have stayed here in the past." Anxious to change the subject, he said to Helen, on whom this last part was lost, "Roberts knew that I set out this morning with the intention of indulging in a little quiet fishing, but I seem to have strayed from my purpose."

She flushed deeply with a painful color that spread down her neck. "I am sorry to be the cause of it, sir."

"You misunderstand me," he told her gently. "There was nothing to prevent me from setting out later. I remained because I chose to." Observing that Vanessa's hunger seemed to have been assuaged, he rose to his feet. "Can I persuade you both to investigate the countryside in my company? The village itself is not particularly worthy of your attention, but providing you are not afraid of cows there is some pleasant scenery to be enjoyed from the river."

Helen shook her head. "I should like it above all things, but I think I ought not to venture out just yet." She added quickly, "But Vanessa must go. I should be uncomfortable if she were to stay behind on my account."

They both looked toward her and as she opened her lips to refuse, Mr. Travers said, "I claim it as a reward for my services this morning!"

"Very well, provided we are not away too long. Let

me change into some walking shoes and I will join you again."

She was away for some time, but finally reappeared, her light sandals replaced by half boots of yellow kid and a straw bonnet tied over her locks by a yellow bow. Mr. Travers, who had been chatting easily with Helen in her absence, excused himself when he saw she had returned to the hall and went out to join her.

She was waiting near the door of the taproom and she fell into step beside him, saying after a small pause, "It was kind in you to invite Helen as well."

"What's this?" He raised his brows in mock surprise. "Atonement?"

"Perhaps. I will admit that I misjudged you. I am so accustomed to the usual reaction to Helen's disability that I tend to become indignant in advance. If only people would realize that she is embarrassed by their pity! I find it so infuriating, particularly when they talk to her in hushed tones as though her understanding were limited as well!"

"I confess that my first reaction was one of pity," Mr. Travers said matter-of-factly, "but I soon decided that it was wasted. Your sister is fortunate in that she has most attractive features and a sweetness of disposition that is at once likable. If she was without her lameness but had a squint and bad teeth instead, she would be an object not of pity but of mockery. Besides, I think you are over sensitive on her behalf. I did not invite her out of conscious kindness. It was merely that her lameness did not strike me as severe enough to preclude a stroll."

After a moment while she digested this, she said in a flattened voice, "Then I do most sincerely beg your pardon, but believe me, your attitude is not the general one."

"You must be unfortunate in your friends! Though I recall you have already said as much. Your sister's illness this morning, however, I do regard as serious. Does she have these attacks often? You seem to deal with them very competently."

"There have been several recently," she replied, her face clouding over. "This last one was definitely aggravated by the travel, but I have noticed that they are invariably brought on by anxiety. The doctor says it is asthma."

"I thought so. I had a great-aunt who suffered from it. You will be relieved to learn that it gradually disappeared and she lived to be seventy-eight, to the frequently expressed disappointment of my uncle. One cannot blame him—she was not a lovable woman."

She looked up, scanning his face. "Is that true, or are you only saying it to comfort me?"

"Perfectly true, on my honor! She died only a few months ago and no one had heard a wheeze from her in years!" He smiled at her encouragingly. "Are you prepared to trust yourself with me through the fields? I assure you I am a gentleman to the core."

"I know," she returned, accepting his hand over a stile. "I questioned the landlord on your character before we set out. Discreetly, of course."

Amused, he said, "So that is why you were so long! What admirable forethought! I am relieved to discover that I passed the test."

"Oh, he told me you were well known to him. I gained the impression that an honor had been conferred on me."

"Flattering," he murmured. "Did he say anything else?"

"No. Why should he?"

"No reason. I was going to wallow in gratification if there was anything else of a complimentary nature, that is all." He guided her down on to the footpath. "I see you do not regard the cows with any qualms."

"It would be strange if I did. We were surrounded by them at home."

"Were? That has an air of finality!"

"Yes." She took a deep breath, remembering their departure the previous evening when she had looked around for the last time at the peeling, damask wall hangings and the filmed crystals of the great chandelier in the beautifully proportioned dining room. Stripped of all its furnishings, their home's years of neglect had been shockingly apparent in the black damp marks rising up from the floor and the patches on the walls where the paintings had been removed.

The view from the windows had presented the same evidence of decline. The sweep of graveled drive was rutted and choked with weeds, though beyond the railings the placidly grazing cattle kept the parkland free of all save nettles and buttercups, which in the distance hazed over the green with their golden yellow. Taking in the familiar scene, she had suffered a momentary pang of regret, but before she could indulge in sentiment the doctor had arrived to take them to catch the Mail.

As the sedate old pony took them around the last bend in the drive, she and Helen had turned to look back at the only home they had ever known. From a distance it was not possible to see the broken windows and missing tiles, and warmed by the sunlight it seemed still the impressive country residence it had once been. Helen had been unable to check her tears, but Vanessa had been almost ashamed to find that her own reaction was one of immense relief.

She became aware that Mr. Travers was watching her, and said, "It seems odd to think we shall never return but you must not suppose that I left it with any sorrow—I feel more as though I have escaped from a prison." She added lightly, "But all this is nothing to do with you. Other people's problems are invariably tedious."

"I wonder if that was intended to put me in my place," Mr. Travers mused. She made a quick gesture of denial, and he said, "I told you I was vulgarly curious. Tell me, did you depart from your erstwhile home with nothing more than was carried into the inn this morning?"

"Of course not! The rest of our belongings have been sent on to Brighton by carrier!"

"Ah, Brighton! I feel it is the crux of the matter. What *are* your intentions when you reach there, apart from enjoying the salubrious effects of the sea air?"

His tone was lightly teasing, but when she paused to look up at him, her face was serious. "To find Helen a husband."

They had by now reached the banks of the river and he leaned forward and skimmed a stone across the water, scattering the minnows. "A laudable ambition," he said slowly. "It seems to me, however, that the matter should not be your responsibility. I judge you have no parents, but surely you have relatives who would concern themselves with your welfare?"

"No," she replied simply. "My father died when we were small, leaving us with hardly any money, and they did not trouble themselves over us then so why should they now? To be absolutely fair, they knew Papa was a gambler, so I don't blame them for not assisting us when he was alive for it was obvious what he would do with it, but they must have known the straits we were in afterward. I think they prefer to forget we exist."

"And your mother?"

"She died last year." She smiled briefly. "But we have managed, and you are not to be feeling desperately sorry for us, if you please! Mama had been . . . difficult . . . for many years before she was taken ill, and there was not that degree of affection between us that one might expect. We have always had our old nanny to cosset us, but she could not accompany us now because her mother is very elderly and she felt it would be wrong of her to move so far away."

Mr. Travers nodded, his pity aroused by this loveless upbringing.

"But you informed your mother's relatives?"

"Oh, yes! They are in Ireland and I wrote to them on her death, but they haven't replied." At his expression of surprise, she said, "The fact of the matter is that she eloped because they wouldn't give their consent to the betrothal, and I don't think a word was ever exchanged between them afterward."

"Orphans cast upon the world," Mr. Travers commented. He warded off an inquisitive cow and tested the grass with his hand. "Shall we sit down? The ground is completely dry." He waited while she settled and spread her muslin skirts about her feet. "Have you no one else? I seem to recall some Hartlands in Yorkshire."

"Yes, there are, but I doubt if they even know of

us," she said candidly. "My father had the misfortune to be the youngest son of a youngest son, and one cannot expect them to show an interest in every little twig of their family tree! Believe me, I have been through all this myself! We are really quite alone, and since the only education we received was from our mother we have no means of earning our living, except as a companion or something of that nature. If anything happened to me, how could Helen cope? With these bouts of asthma she must have the security of marriage, and truthfully I believe that if she had no worries and a kind and considerate man to care for her, her illness would cease altogether."

"It would be best for her, certainly," Mr. Travers said. "What of yourself?"

Humor not quite masking the determination in her eyes, she said airly, "Oh, I have higher ambitions! I shall find myself a wealthy merchant, the richer the better! Mama was the daughter of an earl, you see, and I am informed that that counts for a great deal with persons when they are desirous of entering society!"

"Such cynicism in one so young! There are other things in life besides money."

"Not when you have been all your life without it!" Vanessa retorted. "And I have every intention of giving good value to my merchant. I shall advertise my aristocratic connections and be a decorative addition to his drawing room." Gazing down into the water, she added dreamily, "And in return I shall have a carriage and pair and velvet curtains in all the salons."

"Some brocades are far more expensive," Mr. Travers informed her in a helpful spirit.

"Then I shall hang them in the kitchens if the fancy takes me!"

This was stated with a defiant air, and laughing outright, Mr. Travers said, "You would be well served if you found he had acquired his wealth by practicing the strictest economy!"

Vanessa shook her head firmly. "I should make sure he was wealthy *and* open handed!"

"It would be wise! Does Miss Helen acquiesce in all these plans for the future?"

She wrinkled her nose. "We-ll, to be honest, no. She is of a more nervous disposition and shrinks from drastic remedies. But we *could* not just sit at home until the place fell down about our ears! I had the good fortune to find a man who was willing to pay far more for it than it was worth, so I accepted his offer with gratitide. After that," she dimpled suddenly, "we could not stay in the district. I'm afraid he was rather a vulgar person and our neighbors became hostile when it was discovered what I had done."

Mr. Travers shook with silent laughter. "You are completely unscrupulous! The poor man will be frozen out by the local gentry within the year!"

"I don't think so," she said, a shade guiltily. "He seemed very well able to take care of himself. And where else would I find a buyer? I know Mama tried to sell it before it was in near so bad a state and no one would have it! This man was so ecstatic over the steps and Ionic columns at the front of the house that he was quite prepared to overlook the fact that the rest of the house was falling apart with damp and neglect! Only two of the downstairs rooms and two of the bedrooms were fit for occupation, and for myself, I have the greatest objection to sharing my food with the mice and the cockroaches! Fortunately we had a couple of ruined summerhouses and some very fine cedars in the park. I let it for grazing to a local farmer, so that in spite of the nettles it looked quite presentable. He was most impressed."

Mr. Travers leaned back against a tree and continued to watch her with enjoyment. "I'm told donkeys are excellent for removing nettles. Or was it thistles? I can't remember."

"It's of no consequence now. I daresay he will have them scythed down. He seemed very full of plans and said it wanted naught but money to put it to rights. His daughter is shortly due to leave her finishing school and he told me he wanted a suitable background for her after her fine education."

"And if he was satisfied, why should you throw a rub in his way," Mr. Travers commented.

"My dear sir, our own need was by far the greater! If we had stayed on after Mama died, I could see us dwindling into old maids with Helen getting worse and worse! When this Mr. Porter offered to buy the house it seemed like divine guidance, or at any rate," she amended, "I decided to regard it as such! I wrote at once to an agent to procure us lodgings for the summer months. So now," she spread her hands expressively, "I have burned our boats!"

"You felt no anxiety at the step you were taking?"

"Of course I did! I don't think we have been above thirty miles from home before, and when Helen became ill . . ." She lapsed into a thoughtful silence. "When we resume our journey I think it will be best if we take it in easy stages and stay two or three nights on the road."

"And meanwhile," he said, regarding her lazily from

under half-closed lids, "you and Miss Helen may give me the pleasure of your company for a few more days."

"What of your own plans?"

"I am but a simple country gentleman," Mr. Travers replied untruthfully. "My time for the moment is my own, and the trout may enjoy a brief extension of their liberty."

"Poor things!"

He raised his brows. "Would you express the same sentiment if they were placed before you grilled in butter?"

Laughing, she got to her feet. "I am exposed a hypocrite! I could eat one now!"

"Then we will return for luncheon and see how your sister fares."

He assisted her up the bank and they walked back companionably to the inn where he parted from her in the hall and went into the taproom. It was deserted except for the landlord, and Mr. Travers settled himself comfortably by the counter and requested a tankard of cool ale.

"Anything else I can do for you, sir?" Roberts asked, passing it across.

"Yes." Mr. Travers contemplated his ale for a moment, then looked up with a grin. "You can lend me the gig you keep for your wife."

Roberts halted in the act of wiping the counter. "And why, if I may make so bold as to ask, would you be wanting my gig when your curricle is taking up more room than I can spare in the coach house and those two bays are eating their heads off in the stables?"

Meeting his baffled gaze, Mr. Travers said, "Keep

them hidden. I am a gentleman of modest means taking a fishing holiday . . ."

"Are you then," Roberts interrupted, heavily sarcastic.

"So I shall want to borrow your old chestnut mare as well," Mr. Travers finished.

Roberts raised his eyes to heaven. "Queerest way *I've* ever seen to go about impressing a female! She was in this morning asking about you," he added.

"I know. I hope you didn't tell her of my, er, connections in the district!"

"No," Roberts returned repressively. "Nor I didn't tell her as how I used to hold your head under the pump in the backyard so that you could go home sober when you were a lad. I reckoned it was none of her business. It's none of mine either, but it has me in a puzzle as to why you should be wanting my gig to chase a strange female here when there's company waiting for you up at the Court! One of your footmen was in the back last night and he said your ma-in-law was as mad as fire you hadn't turned up. I didn't let on you were here, but as I said, it has me in a puzzle."

Draining his tankard, Mr. Travers gave him an enigmatic smile. He appeared to be singularly undisturbed by the news of his stepmother's rage.

"Call it midsummer madness," he said.

Chapter Two

In their room, Vanessa cast off her bonnet and smiled down at Helen who was resting on the bed. "How have you been?"

"Perfectly well, I assure you. It has passed off completely and I shall be quite fit to travel again."

Vanessa studied her. There was still a hint of heaviness about her eyelids and she had not fully regained her color. "We will stay a day or two to be certain. It was a mistake to try to do the whole journey in one, and I blame myself for not having realized it beforehand."

Helen said worriedly, "I am only fearful in case it should prove to be expensive here. It is a posting house, after all."

"Oh, well," Vanessa unlaced her half boots and slid her feet out. "If it is, we shall just have to cut short our stay in London. I daresay we can as well buy the things we need in Brighton. Do you wish to go down to luncheon? Mr. Travers has invited us to join him again."

"How kind of him. He is most truly the gentleman, don't you think?" She gave a shy smile and Vanessa stared at her.

"I do believe he has caught your interest! Though when I come to think of it, we have seen no one but the doctor and the vicar who were under sixty, so it would be a wonder if he didn't! Get up and I'll dress your hair again. We haven't had anyone to practice our charms on since we were of an age to be aware of them!"

As Helen made inarticulate noises of protest, she said, "Don't be missish! Who knows but that he may be the very man you have been waiting for. Romance can flower in the unlikeliest of places. At least I've always been given to understand it can. I've never had an opportunity to witness it!"

"Vanessa! I'm sure he had no such thoughts! Besides, he is very likely married. He must be quite thirty."

Vanessa stood, the hairbrush poised. "Good gracious! I wonder why that never occurred to me?" She resumed her brush strokes. "In any event, he told me while we were out that you had most attractive features!"

Color creeping up her cheeks, Helen lowered her eyes. "I haven't asked. Did you have a pleasant morning?"

"Most agreeable—going for a walk with a handsome man is a new experience for me! I all but told him our life history—I can't think why, except that he has a sympathetic face." Expertly, she looped Helen's hair into a soft wave on each side of her face and fastened the curls on the back of her head. "Where are your earrings?"

She stood with the door half open as Helen paused to hook them in, and they heard sounds of a commotion below them. With undisguised curiosity she went on to the landing to discover what it was about, and between the balusters was afforded an excellent picture of the hall and front door of the inn. Through this swept a tall, striking woman, on whose improbably red hair reposed a white satin hat with a ruby lining. Under one arm she carried a black poodle, his dusty paws scrabbling at the rich velvet of her pelisse as he struggled to get down.

With an exasperated exclamation she set him on his feet and turned back to the door, outside of which an enraged male voice was uttering impassioned complaints.

"You're making a fuss over nothing!" she called impatiently.

"I warn you, Patty, you get that damned dog trained or he can run behind the coach on the way back! I'll not do another journey in something that stinks like a kennel! God only knows why you couldn't leave him behind, and that turtle-faced maid with him!"

Her powerful contralto voice rising, she yelled, "Don't you dare call Bess turtle-faced! She's been my dresser these ten years, and where I go, she goes, and so does Jason!"

Emboldened by the mention of his name, Jason came out from under the train of her pelisse and stood aggressively facing the door. A series of shrill yelps erupted from him as the gentleman entered with a swirl of his caped driving coat.

He regarded the animal with malevolence, and said jeeringly, "Aye, you can be brave enough when you're sheltering behind a woman's skirts!"

To refute this, Jason rushed forward, his lips curled up, and the gentleman raised his elegantly booted foot to ward him off.

"You harm a hair of him and Bess and I leave on the instant!" Patty shrieked.

Gloomily, he said, "If I'm to share my stay with Bess and that miserable cur, I'll not stop you! And come to think of it, as *I* remember it, I never invited you in the first place! It was you who insisted on coming! And if you don't want me to do that creature an injury, then keep him out of my way!" He glared at Jason, who once more dived for the shelter of his mistress's pelisse, and glanced about him impatiently. "Let's get the baggage into the rooms. Landlord!"

His drumroll on the desk obtaining no response, he thrust open the door of the tap and repeated his shout. Of Roberts there was no sign, but the Angel's two resident terriers, peacefully sleeping off the effects of a rat hunt, awoke to his call and surged into the hall.

Pandemonium broke out immediately. Jason uttered a squeal of panic, and the terriers, the white hair on their necks raised like ruffs, launched into an organized and businesslike attack. One cut off Jason's retreat from the door while the other, with a series of short rushes, maneuvered him into a corner. In the midst of it all, Patty, with yells of fright, swung about her indiscriminately with her parasol, and the gentleman, laughing heartily, leaned on the door of the tap and spurred on the terriers with shouts of encouragement.

It took Patty a moment to realize that his cries of "That's it! Go at it!" were directed not at herself but at the hunters. Her parasol described a murderous arc that missed his head by only a fraction as she pursed his retreating figure into the tap. Almost helpless with laughter, he raised his arms in an attempt to protect himself.

"Stop it, Patty, and go and rescue that damned dog! Who's going to pay your reckoning here if you slaughter me!"

It was fortunate that Roberts arrived at this point, Jason being in desperate need of rescue. With a well-coordinated pincer movement, the terriers were advancing for the kill and his expectation of life could be measured in seconds.

Roberts dispersed them with a curt order and a shove from his foot, and with a last regretful glance at the petrified poodle, they returned to their resting place behind the bar. Roberts, after watching the spectacle in the tap for a while, said woodenly, "Can I help you, sir?"

Patty's rage dropped away on the instant. With regal dignity she stalked back into the hall and her victim resumed an upright posture.

Grinning, the gentleman ran his fingers through his disordered hair. "Pendril's the name. You have a booking for Miss Morgan and her maid, but I shall want rooms for myself and my valet."

"Ah, yes, my lord," Roberts said, his face still expressionless. "I regret that I have only the one bedchamber spare, but if Miss Morgan would be willing to share with her maid, I shall be able to accommodate you." Ignoring the ludicrous dismay this pronouncement evoked, he went on, "I apologize for the unfortunate occurrence just now, but we were not expecting a dog."

Making a recovery, Lord Pendril said, "Neither was I, my dear fellow, neither was I! And what is more," he added, warming to the idea, "you may poison it with my very good will! Now for God's sake give me a glass of ale! I've near split my sides from laughing!"

Immune to the ways of the quality, Roberts bowed. "If you will give me a few moments to have the lady taken to her bedchamber, I will attend to it, my lord."

Lord Pendril nodded, and sprawled on the settle beside the empty hearth. This movement brought him face to face with Mr. Travers, of whose presence he had not previously been aware. Recognition lighting his features, he exclaimed, "Good God! So this is where you were!"

"What," Mr. Travers demanded, amusement and caution equally blended in his tones, "are *you* doing here?"

"Went to visit you, old man," Lord Pendril returned irrepressibly. "Drove smack up to your front door, baggage and all, only you weren't there!"

"In the name of heaven, you never took Patty to the Court! My stepmother would have hysterics!"

"She was already having 'em when I got there! Seems she was expecting you a few days back. Got a very haughty young beauty there who all but snarled at me when she found I was a friend of yours. Quite frightened me I assure you! Got the impression I was unwelcome all around, so I bolted for here!"

"So did I," Mr. Travers said resignedly. "My revered stepmother has this fixed ambition to see me married, and indefatiguably produces a selection of females who think they might like to be wedded to my money.

She informs me that she had a yearning to see her grandchildren before she dies. I have pointed out that any issue of mine would bear no blood relationship to her, that she is in excellent health, and that she would be better employed in getting Caroline married off, but all to no avail. Fortunately I was forewarned of her latest hope in the nick of time." He grinned suddenly. "You may take my place there with my blessing and please your father at the same time. Elizabeth's a handsome girl and her lineage is impeccable."

"Elizabeth who?" Lord Pendril inquired, ignoring the latter part of this advice.

"Gnosill. She's old Wrenshaw's daughter."

"My God, I thought her face was familiar!" Lord Pendril exclaimed, sitting up straight. "She's the one my mother wanted me to offer for. Swore my old man would come over handsomely if I did, but I couldn't face it." Meditatively, he added, "Next time I get involved it will be with a biddable woman. Patty's an entertaining wench but she exhausts me!"

"Not to mention all those around her! Don't think me inhospitable, Charles, but what brings you to Northamptonshire at this season? You are not usually drawn to the rural scene."

"Can't move in London for the duns!" Lord Pendril replied, with engaging frankness.

Since the noble earl, Lord Pendril's sire, had noted while his heir was still at Harrow that he was possessed of a disturbingly volatile disposition, he had attempted to put a curb on him in his adult years by keeping him on a very limited allowance. Unfortunately, in addition to this means of teaching his son economy, he had decided to pay the money not quarterly but annually in the belief that Lord Pendril would learn to husband his resources. The fact that after nine years it was obvious his hopes were unlikely to be fulfilled, he ignored. Lord Pendril, on this allowance, which he did not hesitate to term miserly, lived in a state of perpetual insolvency. Far from living within his means, he had merely become expert at dealing with creditors.

"If you could do with a little something to tide you over . . ." Mr. Travers offered.

"Thank you, dear boy, and I'll bear it in mind, but I've got a house leased in Brighton next week. I just thought that in the meantime it might be more peaceful at the Court. I hadn't intended bringing Patty of course—she was going on to Brighton when the theatre closes, but she had a row with the manager so I booked her in here. What I didn't bargain for were Jason and the ever-faithful Bess! Ah, well." With a fatalistic shrug he rose to his feet and thumped on the counter. "Where's that landlord?"

"He has Patty to cope with," Mr. Travers reminded him.

Deciding his thirst could wait no longer, Lord Pendril went behind the bar to serve himself and inadvertently stepped on a sleeping terrier. It retaliated by sinking its teeth into his boot and he shook it off good humoredly. "Game little fellows, aren't they? Pity to spoil their sport just now." Drawing a tankard of ale, he raised his brows inquiringly.

Mr. Travers shook his head. "Not for me. I'm entertaining two ladies to luncheon."

"I thought there must be something to keep you here!"

"No, no. They only arrived this morning. I was

merely lurking here until I get word that the Court is clear again."

"Or until your stepmother discovers where you are," Lord Pendril said significantly. "What of these two females?"

Mr. Travers stared reflectively into the middle distance. "They are sisters. One is the loveliest creature I have ever set eyes on. Which reminds me, Charles, you will oblige me by not mentioning my circumstances. I wish it to be thought that I am of limited means and I am simply taking a fishing holiday here."

Lord Pendril swiveled an intelligent eye. "If you say so, dear boy, though they can't all be after your money. Still, if that's the case I'd best go and prime Patty. That wench never could keep her mouth shut. Comes of being on the stage!" He rubbed the terrier down its rough back and was rewarded by a soulful look and a quiver of the short tail. "If I get the chance you can have that black demon for your breakfast," he promised, and went out into the hall.

Since his method of discovering the whereabouts of Patty's room was to stand still and roar her name at the top of his voice, it was hardly surprising that these tactics brought Mrs. Moorcroft and her attendant into the open as well as Vanessa and Helen, who had previously retreated lest they be caught spying.

Mr. Travers, following Lord Pendril out, caught their eye and crooked his arm in invitation. With an urbane bow to the censorious Mrs. Moorcroft, he ushered them into the private parlor, but before he could do more than exchange greetings with them, Lord Pendril's tall frame filled the doorway.

Immediately behind him, Roberts said disapprov-

ingly, "Covers have been laid for you in the main
dining room, my lord."

Unrepentant, Lord Pendril said, "Yes, I know they
have, but I'm not sitting down to a meal with that
sour-faced old harridan watching every mouthful!"

Betrayed into a chuckle, Vanessa drew his attention
for the first time and he swept a bow to both ladies.
"You don't mind if we join you in here?"

Mr. Travers closed his eyes, momentarily overcome
at the thought of the exuberant Patty, and Lord Pendril pulled him back into the hall.

"It will be all right! Patty was in a society play the
other week. I'll tell her to play the duchess! One thing
I will say for that girl, she's a damned fine actress!"

With strong doubts of her ability to sustain the role,
Mr. Travers returned to the Misses Hartland. It struck
him that in exposing two gently bred girls to the influence of London's most likable rake and his current
mistress he was failing in his duty, but for the moment there seemed no help for it.

"Lord Pendril is bringing Miss Morgan down," he
said. "She is . . ." He hesitated, searching for an acceptable description, and encountered Vanessa's eyes,
brimming with merriment.

"Yes, I gathered she was! I assure you, Mr. Travers,
that we have no objection. In fact, having spent all
our lives in seclusion, it is time we embarked on a social education!"

Before Mr. Travers could reply that acquaintance
with Patty would not be generally regarded as a desirable aspect of their tutelage, Lord Pendril brought her
into the parlor, vociferously objecting to Jason's inclu-
sion at the table.

"I can't leave him upstairs unless Bess is with him!"

Seeing that Lord Pendril, for once obtuse, was about to demand why she couldn't, she said hurriedly, choosing her words with care out of respect for the company, "You have complained often enough!"

Lord Pendril scowled at Jason, who, secure under Patty's arm, lifted his lip. "Then lock him in a stable where it doesn't matter!"

Affronted, she clasped the poodle to her bosom, and Mr. Travers intervened to perform the necessary introductions before Lord Pendril could become more particular in his objections.

Soon the ladies were seated at the table, Patty playing her duchess part to perfection, Vanessa watching the new arrivals with barely concealed amusement, and Helen, rather to Mr. Travers's surprise, joining in the conversation with an animation he had not observed in her before. Previously he had thought her lovely but insipid. She had seemed to lack character, but he reflected that this could well have been the result of her illness, and her natural disposition was only just displaying itself. Helping her to cold chicken, he addressed a light remark to her and a tinge of color crept up her cheeks as she raised her head to reply.

From the other side of the table, Vanessa perceived this with dismay. Helen's shyness, so great as to be a positive affliction, had always held her completely tongue-tied in company before, yet under Mr. Travers's gentle persuasion she was talking freely, and, as she watched, Vanessa's uneasiness increased. Impressed by Mr. Travers's pleasant manners and obvious air of breeding, she thought him, so far as she could judge on such brief acquaintance, to be the very type of man she would have chosen for Helen. Her words that morning, however, had only been intended

to give Helen a little more confidence in herself and
she did not seriously believe for a moment that anything could come of a chance encounter at an inn. In a
day or so they would be going their separate ways
and unless Helen in that short time should make a
very deep impression, it has highly unlikely that they
would ever meet again.

But if Helen should attract his notice . . . Her
mind running on ahead, she checked herself. After all,
they knew nothing of him and she could not simply
ask. She recalled that Mr. Travers, in his introduction,
had described Lord Pendril as a boyhood friend, and
she was just wondering if it would be possible to elicit
some information from him when that gentleman decided that the repast laid before them was insuffi-
cient for one who had not breakfasted on the road.
Cold meats and fruit were all very well, he informed
Helen, but not for someone who had an overwhelming
appetite for a hot pie.

Accordingly, he stood up and pulled the bell, an innocent enough action if Roberts had not been busy in
another part of the inn. By ill fortune the summons
was answered by a waiter who had not witnessed the
interesting arrival of the new guests, and in his ignorance he let in the terriers. These, either from an in-
nate prepossession for Lord Pendril's society, or se-
duced by his promise to present them with Jason for
their breakfast, had been snuffling under the door.
The second it was opened, they hurtled through.

Her role of duchess cast to the four winds, Patty let
out a scream and stood on her chair with Jason held
aloft; Mr. Travers made a grab for the nearest black-
and-white body and missed, and Vanessa, bending to
intercept the other, was nearly knocked from her feet

as he rushed after his fellow. Lord Pendril's only con-
tribution being to adjure Patty to mind her language,
the terriers re-formed unhindered for another on-
slaught. Trained in ratting from their earliest months
they summed up the situation at a glance and simulta-
neously decided that the tall, Welsh dresser was the
only feasible point of attack. This they reached without difficulty by way of the windowsill, the blue-and-
white china sliding from its polished surface to crash
to the floor as they balanced on the edge preparatory to
launching themselves off.

Here Lord Pendril decided to intervene, not from
any regard for the shivering Jason, but because the
slightest miscalculation on the part of the terriers
would inevitably land them in the middle of the table
and he had not yet finished his luncheon.

As the first one sprang he caught it in midair and
stationed himself squarely in front of Patty in order to
foil its companion.

"Finest fielder in my year at Harrow," he informed
them equably.

The terrier, with flattened ears, was licking him ec-
statically under his chin and he rubbed its head. "Yes,
yes! You're a grand little fellow, and as far as I am
concerned you could have that lily-livered cur and
welcome, but there's no denying it would cause trouble!" Hitching the other one under his arm, he carried
them out to the speechless waiter, and could be heard
promising them some sport in the stableyard later in
the afternoon.

He returned to find all save Patty still shaking with
laughter. She, as Jason's fond owner, was endeavoring
to control her natural reaction to Lord Pendril's indif-
ference to the fate of her pet.

"You!" she exploded.

"Now don't start again, Patty. I saved him, didn't I?"

"Saved him! It was the raspberry tart you were saving! D'you think I don't know you?"

"Well, it worked out the same! Here, stick him on a chair and give him a bit of meat to cheer him up! Never met such a spineless creature in my life!" Suiting the action to the words, he reached out for Jason, who with characteristic ingratitude repaid his savior by biting his finger. Lord Pendril merely sucked it and, seating himself at the table again, remarked, "Now where were we before all the excitement?"

Pulling Patty's chair forward for her since Lord Pendril had neglected this performance of his duties, Mr. Travers said, "Charles, why is it that excitement invariably follows you about?"

"Couldn't tell you, dear boy," Lord Pendril said, bestowing very little thought on the matter. "Can't say it bothers me though. It's only the duns trailing me that I object to, and they're a cursed nuisance at times!" Glancing up, he caught the amused sympathy in Vanessa's expression and said, "Don't tell me you're troubled with 'em as well!"

She nodded. "I used to be."

"Well!" he exclaimed. "Shocking bad form to dun the ladies!"

"By no means," she returned, still unable to keep the laughter from her voice. "They are just as entitled to their money from me as from you!"

Unimpressed by this reasonable point of view, he said, "As far as I'm concerned, they can't have what isn't there! They'll just have to chase their tails until I get back from Brighton."

Helen, shocked by this insouciant dismissal of debt, could not decide whether this was of greater moment than his disclosure that he too was going to Brighton. Reaching the conclusion that the moral issues were no concern of hers, she said, "What a coincidence! We are going there also!"

"Really? That's famous! We must all get together again!" He began to ask in what part of the town they were staying, while Mr. Travers told Vanessa that he had made arrangements to borrow the landlord's gig if she and Helen should like to go for a drive when the air was cooler.

"Or this afternoon if you would prefer it," he added.

She shook her head. "To own the truth, I doubt if I could stay awake. We neither of us slept on the coach and I am haunted by visions of my bed. But this evening, when we are rested, we should be delighted to come. I know I can answer for Helen as well."

"Good." He smiled down on her. "Now, can I help you to some of this raspberry tart that Miss Morgan is convinced Lord Pendril was intent on preserving for himself?"

Miss Morgan, deciding that resumption of her society role was now pointless, beamed on them largely. "Call me Patty! I don't care for all this formality, and address Quentin as Mr. Travers after the years I've known him is more than I could bring myself to do!" She received a warning look from Mr. Travers and grinned at him. With the memory that she had enjoyed a six months' spell under his protection, Mr. Traver's frown increased, but she had turned away from him. "Charles, make sure those dogs aren't on the other side of the door! I want to take Jason out before I go upstairs."

With a muttered animadversion to Mr. Travers, Lord Pendril obliged and escorted Patty out. Mr. Travers sat a minute or two longer until Vanessa, stifling her yawns, asked apologetically if he would excuse them before she committed the ultimate solecism of falling asleep in front of him, which she felt herself to be in danger of doing.

Smiling sympathetically, he said, "Until six o'clock then?"

She assented, raising her hand in a farewell salute, and Mr. Travers, with the idea that he could exercise the bays while they were safely in their room, made his way to the stableyard.

He discovered immediately that Lord Pendril was before him. A traveling carriage had pulled in for a change of team, and to one side of it a private chaise was queuing behind one of the Angel's own post chaises for a fresh pair. As the tired carriage team was led off, the coachman was critically inspecting the new horses and checking the harness, and from somewhere inside the stables, a cry of, "Next pair out!" summoned the postboys to the chaise. It was a scene of bustle and activity, and in the middle of it all, Lord Pendril had decided to conduct a rat hunt. He had the covers off two of the drains and was calling for some rods to put down them, while an ostler said despairingly, "But I *told* you, my lord, that we had the ferrets down them only yesterday, and the terriers are promised to the farmer down the road for this afternoon!"

A dingy individual with a squirming bag over one shoulder corroborated this, and Lord Pendril said, "Better still! I'll take them myself!" He whistled to the terriers who came to heel at once, and espied Mr.

Travers. "Coming, Quentin? We're going to have some sport!"

"I was going to take the bays out," Mr. Travers replied, watching with amusement the havoc that his lordship's sporting propensities had already produced in the courtyard.

"Tell you what," Lord Pendril said, flinging an arm across Mr. Travers's shoulders. "You come with me now, and I'll take those bays of yours out tonight."

"There is an old Arabian proverb," Mr. Travers murmured. "Never lend your horse or your wife!"

"I'll treat them as though they were my own!"

"That," Mr. Travers told him, "is what I was afraid of!"

Secure in the knowledge that he was widely accounted an excellent whip, Lord Pendril grinned at him. "Got to do something to keep Patty in a good humor, dear boy—country life isn't precisely her cup of tea—and I'm sure she'd fancy your curricle."

"Very well, but for heaven's sake, take them in the opposite direction from the Court! The bays are well known, and it wouldn't take long for word to reach my stepmother." He gave Lord Pendril a quizzical smile. "Will you acknowledge us if you meet us out in Roberts's gig?"

"What the devil are you?—Ah, I remember, you're of modest means! Good thing none of you are fat if you mean to squeeze three in a gig!" He grinned again. "The younger one's a beauty, by God! I don't think I've ever seen one to equal her!"

"Interested?" Mr. Travers queried.

Lord Pendril shook his head vigorously. "I told you it will be a biddable one the next time. That girl has a bite in her unless I'm mistaken!" He turned to find the dingy little man still patiently regarding him. "Got the ferrets in there? Good man! Lead the way then! Are you coming, Quentin?"

Mr. Travers shrugged tolerantly. "Since you have taken upon yourself the task of exercising my horses . . ."

They turned and walked out of the yard together, much the same height and similar in coloring, both having medium brown hair and brown eyes. Here the resemblance ended, Lord Pendril's mobile face and carelessly extravagant dress being in direct contrast to the quiet humor in Mr. Travers's face, and his unassuming, well-cut clothes. Ahead of them, the terriers, tails aquiver and tongues lolling in the heat, paused every now and again to make sure Lord Pendril was still with them.

Taking note of their adoring expressions, Mr. Travers remarked, "They seem to have attached themselves to you."

Lord Pendril nodded and bent to pick up a stick from under the hedgerow. They stiffened in eager anticipation and were off like two black-and-white streaks before it had left his hand, growling and worrying it as they fought over which one should have the privilege of returning it.

This performance the ferret man regarded in mute puzzlement. In his opinion, working dogs were working dogs and it was senseless to waste time and their energy when there were rats to be caught. He indicated that their goal lay beyond the next field. Here the farmer was so discomposed to find that Mr. Travers, who happened to be his landlord, and with him a real live viscount, proposed to conduct the rat hunt, that after respectfully greeting them he retired in confusion to demand of his wife what refreshments would be in order to lay out for two such exalted visitors. Terror-stricken, she flew to inspect the contents of her larder, but when, toward the end of the afternoon, they invaded her kitchen, it turned out they required nothing but ale.

Hot and dusty, Lord Pendril downed his in one, thereby causing Mrs. Burton severe disappointment. Never having come face to face with a member of the aristocracy before, she had cherished her own picture of them, and the discovery that they shared the same plebeian tastes as her husband's farm laborers was a disillusionment.

She suffered a further shock when she went to turn the terriers out of the kitchen. Lord Pendril not only forbade their expulsion but asked if she had any scraps. These he fed to them with his own hands, heaping lavish praise on them for the afternoon's catch, which had indeed been most satisfactory. With the help of the ferrets they had disposed of five rats in the drains and the granary had yielded a further six. They were laid out in a neat row along the wall outside the cowsheds, and the farmer was cudgeling his brains on how to avoid paying the ferret man for the full eleven tails. It was not, as he afterward informed his wife, that he minded parting with his money. Rats were a plague and he was thankful to be rid of them, but he objected to paying for the six tails in which the ferrets had taken no part, particularly when their owner was a thieving rogue whom he strongly suspected in the matter of his missing hens.

The terriers, meanwhile, as though aware that they owed their continued presence to Lord Pendril, sat at his feet and regarded him with liquid and worshipful

eyes, though as it turned out, their devotion was the
cause of a further disturbance at the Angel later that
afternoon. Mr. Travers, on finishing his ale, consulted
the fob at his waist and realized that if he was to take
a much needed bath, he barely had time to be ready
for the excursion in Roberts's gig. They therefore returned at once to the inn, where Lord Pendril, by
pure chance, discovered that Bess had gone into the
nearest town to purchase some essential item that her
mistress had forgotten to put out for packing. The tap
and public rooms of the inn were busy but the resi-
dential part was still quiet, and he seized the opportunity to pay a discreet visit to Patty's bedchamber. The
terriers, slipping once more out of the tap, tracked the
object of their affection unerringly to this location
and set up quite a scratching and whining to be let in.
On the other side of the door, Jason yelled a shrill
defiance and the noise reached such a pitch that Lord
Pendril was obliged to open it. Minus his coat and
neckcloth and with his cambric shirt undone to the
waist, he was ordering them with some vehemence to
go away, when the door opposite opened and Mrs.
Moorcroft's scandalized face appeared.

She let out a shriek, then gathering herself up, said,
"Disgusting!"

"Oh, mind your own business!" Lord Pendril said
irritably. "Patty, can't you keep that dog quiet?"

From inside the room, Patty shouted, "I like that!"
and Mrs. Moorcroft informed him furiously that she
was going to complain to the landlord.

"Do so by all means!" Lord Pendril retorted. He
slammed the door, this time with the terriers on the
inside, and a fresh uproar immediately broke out. He
reemerged a few moments later, hot and bad tem-

pered, the terriers at his heels, and with his neckcloth over his arm. Regarding the pair in exasperation, he said, "Now look what you've done!"

They cowered down to the floor, ears flattened, and the more venturesome of the two crept forward and crawled up his leg to pleadingly lick his hand. He continued to view it severely, then with a gradual smile rubbed its head and said, "Oh, very well then, go on with you!"

At once they backed off from him, forelegs braced and tails in the air, and with sharp barks of delight, galloped frenziedly twice up and down the corridor before returning to lead him back to his own quarters. Grinning, he followed them, and once in his bedchamber they discovered his recently discarded shirt on the floor and after snuffling over it delightedly, lay down on it in quiet contentment.

His lordship's man, gliding in to help his master change, attempted to retrieve it, but leaped back when faced with a threatening growl from each throat.

Lord Pendril, lowering his chin to achieve the folds in a fresh neckcloth, told him briefly to leave them.

"But they're never going to stay there, my lord!" the valet said, aghast.

"Yes. Why not!"

The valet, who was owed a quarter's wages, took a strong grip on himself. "It is one of your best shirts, my lord, and they appear to be somewhat dirty!"

"So would you be if you'd spent the afternoon down a drain," his lordship informed him. He deftly set the folds on his neckcloth to rights and held out his arms for his coat. "Go down to the stables and ask them to have Mr. Travers's bays put to. I shall want them in half an hour, and mind, if anyone says anything to you, you're to give it out they belong to me!"

Too used to his master's vagaries to even wonder at this, the valet nodded, and Lord Pendril went on. "Then find Bess if she's back and get her to tell Miss Morgan to meet me in half an hour. If I go up to her room myself, that old witch opposite is bound to spot me and set up another screech!"

After a small pause, the valet said, "I have been given to understand, sir, that Miss Morgan is contemplating returning to town!"

This was a masterly understatement, all those within earshot of Miss Morgan's rich, contralto tones being aware that she did not propose to stay at the Angel a minute longer than it took to pack.

Untroubled, Lord Pendril slipped on his signet ring and put his snuffbox in his pocket. "She can't go tonight because the stage has gone through and she hasn't got enough money with her to travel post. She'll have forgotten about it by tomorrow." By way of appeasement, he added, "Tell Bess I said she could bring that damned dog with her if she wants to."

The valet bowed and went off to perform these errands, and after viewing himself in the mirror, Lord Pendril turned back to the terriers.

"You're to stay here!" he told them severely. "I can't have you coming with me again. You've caused enough trouble for one day."

They gazed pathetically up at him, and rendered uncomfortable, he picked up one of his York tan driving gloves and placed it before them. One of them squirmed forward and laid his chin on it and after a small hesitation he gave them the other. "Now you've got one each, and if you chew them . . ." Leaving the threat in the air he let himself out and went down to the hall, where he found Mr. Travers unashamedly eavesdropping with his ear to the door of the public dining.

"If we are judged by the company we keep, I have not one shred of reputation left," he informed Lord Pendril.

"What's toward?"

"Mrs. Moorcroft is regaling the early diners with the tale of the Seduction on the Second Floor!"

Lord Pendril snorted. "I wasn't in there above three minutes!"

"Ah, but she obviously doesn't know that, and I understand that you opened the door in a state of . . . er, undress!"

"She should stay behind her own door, then she wouldn't be offended!" He turned as Roberts came into the hall. "Ah, Landlord, I wanted a word with you!"

"Yes, my lord," Roberts said impassively. "As a matter of fact, I was wondering if I might have a word with you."

"If it's about the old scarecrow in the dining room . . ."

"If I could ask you to be a little more discreet, my lord. I cannot afford to have my other guests incommoded."

"Incommoded!" An unholy grin lit up Lord Pendril's intelligent face. "Let me tell you, my dear fellow, that that woman will not leave this inn while there is the slightest chance of her catching me again! No, what I wanted to ask you was, do those terriers have any names?"

"Not as far as I am aware, my lord, but I will inquire and see if they answer to anything."

"And I shudder to think what it may be," Mr. Travers commented when Roberts had gone. "I think the time is rapidly approaching, Charles, when you will have to choose between those two animals and Patty!"

"Oh, Patty's been restless these last three months," Lord Pendril said cheerfully. "She's a good-hearted girl but . . ." He broke off as the dining-room door opened to reveal Helen and Vanessa, and an expression of dismay settled over his features.

Helen appeared both troubled and embarrassed, but Vanessa regarded him with a twinkle. "I had no idea such wickedness went on in a simple country inn!"

"Ladies born," Mr. Travers murmured, "do not remark of it."

She raised her brows. "Oh! Is that true?"

"Only amongst relatives and close friends over the teacups," he confirmed.

She chuckled. "I will remember! Well, sir, here we are, exactly on six o'clock! I trust you have not neglected to perform your part."

"Of course not." He smiled gently on Lord Pendril. "Though I am afraid Lord Pendril will put us to shame with his turnout. I saw it in the yard just now. A very fine pair of horses."

"Thank you," his lordship replied. Without a blink, he added, "As a matter of fact, I'm not at all sure that Patty intends coming. If she doesn't appear, you may like to borrow it."

"You are very kind," Mr. Travers said with feeling, "but I don't think I should care for the responsibility. Ladies, this way if you please."

He ushered them out to the yard where Roberts himself was standing at the head of the fat cob. In tones devoid of expression, he said, "If I could ask you to bear in mind, sir, that the old mare is close on eighteen?"

Mr. Travers took the reins and grinned at him over the chestnut rump. "I shan't spring her," he promised. Reaching out a hand, he assisted Helen and Vanessa into the gig and suffered a momentary twinge as his own horses were led around the corner, plunging and snorting. He watched as Lord Pendril climbed up behind them, calling to Patty as he did so. She came through the rear door of the inn with Jason tucked under her arm, and since she had chosen to wear a carriage dress in a startling shade of pink, her sudden appearance, coupled with Jason's yapping, caused the bays to rear, lifting the muttering ostler clear from the ground.

With a pained murmur, Mr. Travers handed the reins back to Roberts and went over to the bays. Under his soothing influence they remained quiet enough for Patty to embark. He returned to the gig as Lord Pendril held them to a standstill for a moment under the archway to the yard, then disappeared down the road in a cloud of dust.

The chestnut mare, her blood stirred by the spectacle, reared and attempted to emulate their departure, but recalled by Mr. Travers's firm hands, rounded the bend at a sedate trot. Once on the road he looked sideways at his companions, and found Vanessa watching the receding curricle with overt envy.

"Do you drive, Miss Vanessa?" he inquired.

"I? My dear sir, we haven't owned a horse since I was five years of age! We were forced to give up our carriage and the hacks and ponies when Papa died. Since then I have hardly sat behind anything more exciting than the doctor's horse, and he was due to be retired the moment the doctor could afford another!" She paused, dwelling on inward thoughts. "But when I marry my rich merchant, I shall have just such a pair as those!"

"Vanessa!" Helen's voice held gentle reproof. "She does not mean it, Mr. Travers, I assure you."

"Oh, but I do! Nothing is gained in this world by sentiment. Look at the doctor! If he had not refused to accept a penny of what we owed him, I daresay he could have bought a new horse long ago!"

"Vanessa!" Helen said again. "Mr. Travers, I do not know why she is set on giving you such a picture of herself, but it is far removed from the truth! She took upon herself all the worry of this move to Brighton entirely for my sake, and . . ."

"Nonsense! I could not bear the cockroaches, and the mere thought of spending another winter there was enough to send me into a decline! It was every bit as much for myself!" She stared defiantly at Mr. Travers.

His gaze fixed imperturbably on the road between the old cob's ears, he said, "At least you have answered my next question. I was going to ask if either of you rode."

"Not for the past fourteen years," Vanessa said. "They do say one never forgets how, but we have not had a chance to put the theory to the test."

"Then may I suggest that you do so?" He guided the mare into a quiet lane and slowed her to a walk so that he could turn and look at Helen. "I beg you will not be offended, ma'am, but it occurred to me that perhaps you would feel more confident in the saddle. I have a friend in the district and I could easily arrange to borrow his hacks if you would like it." Watching Helen in case he should have wounded her, he did not see the flash of gratified surprise on Vanessa's face. She glanced across quickly to Helen, whose expression lit up with pleasure, then became downcast as she said, "But we have no habits!"

"I hadn't thought of that," Mr. Travers admitted ruefully. Measuring Vanessa with his eye, he hazarded that she was a little smaller than his sister, so hers would present no problem, but Helen was a good deal taller. He went through the families in the district with whom he was acquainted, and visualized their reaction to the request for a loan of such a garment. Meeting Vanessa's eyes, he said, "I know where I could perhaps, obtain one for you, but Miss Helen . . ." He snapped his fingers. "Unless Patty should have brought one with her. From the quantity of luggage that was carried in, I shouldn't be surprised if she had packed her entire wardrobe!"

Horrified, Helen exclaimed, "But we couldn't possibly . . ."

"Mr. Travers could," Vanessa interrupted dryly.

Helen's face cleared. "Of course! I had forgotten you were well acquainted with Miss Morgan."

It was said entirely without guile and Vanessa bit back the words hovering on her tongue, and instead said, "Is it because you have friends here that you know the district so well?"

Mr. Travers, who had foreseen that he was likely to be greeted by almost everyone he met on the road, agreed to this and, drawing heavily on the history of Lord Pendril's visits to the Court, said he had a boyhood friend from Harrow in the district with whom he had been accustomed to spending many of his holidays. "As a matter of fact I had thought to be there now," he went on, "but I discovered he had been called away suddenly and rather than put his mother to the trouble of entertaining me when she had other guests I put up at the Angel."

"But won't your friend object to your borrowing his horses when he is away from home?" Vanessa protested.

"He is a very close friend," Mr. Travers said firmly. "And he knows I should very willingly do the same if the positions were reversed."

Vanessa took note of the fact that this statement seemed to imply that Mr. Travers kept a number of hacks, while he pondered briefly on how to remove three horses from the stables at the Court without his stepmother and half the staff being aware of it. He decided to exercise his mind on the problem later. The warm summer air and the heavy scent of May blossom from the hedges on either side induced a mellow, carefree mood that discouraged speculation.

Beside him, Helen leaned back, sighing contentedly, and said, "This is very pleasant, Mr. Travers."

"I'm glad the day is ending more agreeably than it began for you." It was a conventional response, but he found he meant it sincerely. No one could help liking Helen, though his feelings for her sister he found harder to define.

Smiling up at him, she said, "I can scarcely believe it was only this morning we arrived."

"Nor can I," he said truthfully, wondering if he had indeed been possessed by midsummer madness, and where it all would end.

Backing the gig into the gateway of a hayfield, he turned toward the post road and they proceeded back to the inn at a leisurely pace, enjoying the light breeze that had sprung up. Just short of their objective, Lord Pendril passed them with a flourish, the bays stepping out in fine style, and by the time they reached the front door of the inn, where Mr. Travers paused for the ladies to alight, the curricle had been put away and its occupants were nowhere in sight.

With a fair idea of Lord Pendril's premier requirements, Mr. Travers made his way to the tap where he found his lordship fending off the terriers' first hysterical greeting.

"Stayed without moving, just where I told 'em to," he informed Mr. Travers proudly.

"Commendable," Mr. Travers replied. "And where was that?"

"On my shirt."

"I almost begin to have sympathy for Patty. How are my bays?"

"Magnificient, dear boy! Magnificient! Barely damp under their collars when I brought them back. Can't think why you're setting up all this caper with the landlord's gig, just for a pair of blue eyes that will be gone from here in a couple of days."

"Violet, Charles, violet," Mr. Travers corrected gently. "And I have formulated a plot to delay them. Where is Patty?"

"Gone to her room." Removing the terriers' paws from his breeches, he told them severely that they were keeping him from his ale.

"And where is her room?" Mr. Travers asked patiently.

Lord Pendril grinned. "Third door along the second

floor. You can't miss it! You'll hear her long before you reach it!"

Patty's voice declaiming lines from a little-known drama smote him as he gained the head of the stairs. Wondering whether the other guests were grateful for this free performance of the histrionic art, he knocked on the door and the oration ceased. Commanding Bess to hold Jason, she opened it a crack and, surprised, said, "Oh, it's you!"

"Don't leave me standing here," Mr. Travers begged. "I feel uncomfortably conspicuous!"

She grinned and retreated to tie Jason's leash to the bedpost. "Come in and tell me what I can do for you, since I doubt it's the same as four years ago."

Mr. Travers winced and closed his eyes. "Must you be so forthright?" Opening them again, he viewed Jason's double row of yellowed teeth. "And let me tell you, Patty, that even if it were, that animal would effectively drive all such thoughts from my mind! Doesn't he prove a disadvantage?"

"He might," Patty admitted. "But I'm thinking of getting married."

"This is very sudden!"

"Not at all! I've been considering it for some time. After all, I'm seven and twenty and it's time I turned respectable."

"Nine and twenty," Mr. Travers corrected, ignoring the dramatic gesture of admission that went with her words. "Who is the fortunate man?"

"None of your business," she returned, tapping him on the chest. "Now what is it that you want? I was just going to change for dinner."

"I wondered if you had a riding habit with you that you would be willing to lend to the Misses Hartland."

"I have and they can borrow it gladly, but it would hang like a sack on the little one. Bess, get it out of the cupboard!"

"It is intended principally for the elder Miss Hartland," Mr. Travers said, watching Bess lay out the garment on the bed, and hoping, without much conviction, that emerald-green velvet accorded with Helen's taste.

"For God's sake, which one are you chasing!" Patty exclaimed, amazed.

"None of your business," Mr. Travers retorted, with some satisfaction.

"Hm." Patty regarded him consideringly. "Unless I'm much mistaken, Charles is beginning to have an interest there!"

"You must be wrong!"

Patty shook her head sagely and propelled him toward the door. "I'm not, but I won't argue with you. Now get along so that I can change. I'll send the habit along to their room."

Pausing in the corridor to thank her, Mr. Travers became aware that Mrs. Moorcroft had fixed him with a denunciatory stare.

"Oh, my reputation," he groaned.

Chapter Three

The problem of the riding habit for Vanessa occupying his thoughts, Mr. Travers once more rose early, and made his way to the stables, where a solitary groom was saddling Roberts's own gray gelding for him. A noted judge of horseflesh, he admirably hid his opinion of the animal so kindly lent to him and, reflecting that beggars could not be choosers, swung himself into the saddle.

However, though lacking in beauty, and almost totally ignorant of the schooling and manners that Mr. Travers considered essential in his own horses, once on the open road the gray proved to be unexpectedly free moving, and Mr. Travers clattered through the still sleeping village with the pleasant superiority of a man who is enjoying a morning ride while everyone else is still abed.

The dawn air was fresh, and setting a brisk pace, he soon arrived at the lodge gates and with no more delay than it took to rouse the lodgekeeper and cross the park, was once more back at the Court.

The sounds of his arrival spared him the necessity of waking Walker, who lived over the stables. As Mr. Travers was leading the gray to the water trough, Walker erupted precipitously into the open, slippers on his feet and a pair of breeches pulled hastily over his nightshirt.

After one startled glance at the gelding he came to a halt and fixed Mr. Travers with an accusing eye. "I thought it was a loose horse at this hour of the morning!"

Mr. Travers grinned. "I want to be away from here again before the others are astir."

"Well, if anyone was to see Landlord's gray they'd never suspect it was you riding him," Roberts said with an audible sniff, as he took the reins.

"Do not judge only by appearances, Walker. He's quite a comfortable ride, though you may have the pleasure of returning him for me. I'll take Orestes." He stood for a moment, tapping his whip against his boot. "I shall want Pandora made ready as well, and . . . has Hussein ever carried a lady's saddle?"

"Miss Caroline's ridden him a couple of times. Says he went quietly enough."

"Has she indeed! No doubt she will explain why when I see her!" He looked up at the stable clock, which proclaimed the hour to be still only half past six. "I wonder what she will say to being woken now?"

Venturing no comment, Walker merely said, "When will you want them ready for?"

"As soon as possible. Plain snaffle bridles and side-saddles on Hussein and Pandora. We're taking them to the Angel, and we leave when I return from seeing Miss Caroline."

Walker regarded him gloomily. "And what am I to say when the lads come on the yard, which they will be soon? I can hardly tell them I'm taking them to the smithy, not with sidesaddles on!"

Mr. Travers raised his brows. "It is no concern of theirs."

"What if the mistress gets wind of it?"

"Pray she doesn't!" Mr. Travers said callously, disappearing in the direction of the house. Here he was fortunate in that the only person he encountered was a susceptible housemaid, and by blandishments and the bribe of a crown he secured both her promise to wake his sister and a vow of undying secrecy. Bobbing endless curtsies, she admitted him to Caroline's room, then fled, wreathed in smiles.

Caroline, heavy-eyed and half in and half out of her wrapper, said sleepily, "Mama will kill you if she finds you back here!"

"I know." Pouring a glass of water, he handed it to her. "See if that will wake you up. Why she can't concentrate her energies instead on ridding herself of you, I cannot imagine!"

"Don't be horrid," Caroline said tolerantly. "You know perfectly well I am to be presented next season. Where have you been hiding?"

"At the Angel down in the village."

She opened her eyes wide in awe. "What a frightful risk! Why have you come back and put your head in the lion's den?"

"I shall cherish that remark and repeat it to your mama if I think the occasion warrants it," Mr. Travers said, surveying her dispassionately. "You're a bag-gage!"

She shook her head at him. "You wouldn't betray me. You never have done yet."

"Nor will I this time if you will do something for me."

"How exciting! Are you in some dreadful trouble?"

"No," Mr. Travers said dampeningly, beginning to wonder if he was showing wisdom in making the re-quest. "I merely want to borrow one of your riding habits."

"Quentin! If you are keeping some dreadful female at the inn and expecting me to . . ."

"I most certainly am not!" Mr. Travers interrupted. "I don't know any dreadful females, and if I did, I shouldn't lodge them at Priors Cross!"

"Well, Lady Wrenshaw said Lord Pendril had one in his carriage when he called, and she hinted that you used to . . ."

"That will do, miss! I'm quite sure she didn't say it in front of you! You've been listening at doors again!"

"But Mama said," Caroline continued gaily, ignor-ing him, "that all that was past and you were *entirely* sensible and dependable now, and she didn't know how Lord Pendril could have the effrontery!" Her eyes took on a faraway look as she dwelt for a mo-ment on Lord Pendril, and Mr. Travers was conscious of a warning bell somewhere in the back of his mind. Withdrawing her gaze from the wall, she said, "Whom do you want my riding habit for, then?"

Mr. Travers sighed, realizing that nothing but a de-gree of truthfulness would serve. "Two young ladies have been forced to break their journey at the Angel, and since they are likely to be delayed for a few days,

I offered them the use of my horses. Unfortunately they have no riding habits with them. Does that satisfy you, miss?"

"Mama was right," Caroline said sapiently. "She said that left to yourself you would choose someone completely ineligible!"

"My dear Caroline, you have an overfertile imagination! As I have already said, they are merely breaking their journey and will be gone in a short while."

With polite skepticism, she asked, "In that case, why don't you wish to borrow *two* habits?"

"Simply because I have already managed to obtain one!"

"Hah!" Caroline exclaimed, pouncing on this last. "So that female *is* there!"

Too late Mr. Travers recalled that however lacking she might be in scholastic achievement, his sister had always been undesirably quick witted in other respects. "Yes," he admitted. "But her presence has absolutely nothing to do with me!"

Caroline nodded again, not doubting him. Her mind was busily working out that if Patty's continuance at the inn was not on her brother's account, then it must be on Lord Pendril's. "I'll find a habit and Thomas can carry it with him when he comes down with the post. I trust this young lady—who is only breaking her journey—won't split it at the seams!"

"Why don't you ask me for a description outright?" Mr. Travers inquired amiably. "She is, I should say, a little smaller than you both in height and in build, she has very dark hair and a generally pleasing appearance. The other lady, in case you are interested, is her sister, and though she is taller, they are very much alike." Caroline made a face at him, and he continued,

"And as I should prefer that Thomas remained in ignorance of my whereabouts, I will take the habit with me now."

"Heavens! You don't suppose I should be simpleton enough to address it to you, do you?" she said airily. "I shall have it parceled up and tell him to give it to the landlord. You have only to tell him you are expecting it and all will be well. Thomas comes down midmorning, so it will give me more time to sort one out and make sure it is in order."

Eyes suddenly narrowed, Mr. Travers said, "I cannot imagine your mama employing a maid who did not ensure that your clothes were kept in order at all times!"

"Oh, Florence is *most* efficient, but she is having to wait on Elizabeth as well," Caroline replied, improvising shamelessly. "Her maid has developed the most dreadful summer cold, so poor Florence is continually running between us. But don't worry—I shall have it ready in time."

Still suspicions, Mr. Travers said, "Thank you," but she met his searching gaze limpidly, and experience told him there was little likelihood of obtaining satisfaction by further questioning; so he merely said, "You may now go back to sleep," and let himself out.

In the stables he managed to intercept Walker without being seen and asked him if he was ready to leave.

The head groom said he was, adding that he had hidden the horses behind the big barn. "But I'll tell you now," he said glumly, "Landlord's gray won't lead and he keeps trying to kick the others. On top of which, I've the extra horse for me to ride back on."

"I see no problem," Mr. Travers said. "I will lead

Hussein and Pandora and you may then concentrate on making sure he doesn't kick the spare horse."

It was a solution that deeply offended Walker's sense of what was fitting, but as events turned out, was the means of saving Mr. Travers. Their route at one point took them dangerously close to the house, and glancing up, Mr. Travers saw his stepmother looking out of her bedroom window. He stiffened, but she betrayed no interest, obviously presuming him to be one of the undergrooms. Hardly daring to hope that he could escape recognition, he kept his head averted until they had rounded the corner into the park.

Out of sight, Walker let out his pent-up breath. "That was lucky!"

"Lucky but lowering," Mr. Travers said acidly. Meeting Walker's inquiring gaze, he said, "Not only would it imply that I must have a singularly unmemorable countenance, but that my tailor's efforts are readily mistaken for the garb of a stableboy!"

A rare smile lit Walker's face as he studied Mr. Travers's riding coat, which sat without a crease across his shoulders. "The mistress's eyes aren't what they were," he said soothingly. "Though if it had been my Lord Pendril now, I'd take bets she'd have recognized him straight off!"

In this he was probably correct, as Lord Pendril was that morning attired in a coat of a distinctly more noticeable shade of green than the current, fashionable olive, and had, moreover, chosen to wear it over a waistcoat with vertical stripes. At first only the terriers received the benefit of this eye-catching ensemble, since Lord Pendril had also risen at an unaccustomed hour. In the absence of his usual evening pastimes he had sought his bed at an earlier hour than was his wont, and consequently found himself awake with the birds and with no one to talk to. He therefore took the terriers on an extensive and invigorating run, in the course of which they fell foul of several farm dogs, returning for his breakfast well before the hour when he normally opened his eyes.

Over a large plateful of grilled ham he learned from Roberts that Mr. Travers had set out for the Court without saying when he expected to be back. Since Patty never emerged from her room before noon when she could avoid it, and he was by nature gregarious, he conceived the happy notion of asking the Misses Hartland to accompany him on a gentle tour of the village and its environs. The invitation was issued to Vanessa, whom he encountered in the entrance hall, and was accepted by her with alacrity as it provided a useful opportunity to discover various things that she was burning to know.

For some time the previous evening her mind had turned on Mr. Travers and his very surprising offer to take them riding. Totally inexperienced as she was of the ways obtaining in the world outside her home village, it still did not seem an action one would expect in a chance-met gentleman in a posting house, and she began for the first time to seriously indulge the hope that he had formed an interest in Helen. The next step, plainly, was to ascertain whether Helen nursed a like sentiment in respect of Mr. Travers, but to do so delicately so as not to arouse any suspicion of what she was about. Intimately acquainted with Helen's sensitive nature, she knew it would be fatal at this stage to let fall the smallest hint. Helen would at once retreat into herself, morbidly aware of her limp and what she believed to be her social shortcomings, and that would be the end of any possibility of a happy outcome. Vanessa knew well enough that in company her sister's reticence made her appear dull, and bitterly blamed her mother for fostering this drawback. Lady Mary, titled and beautiful, and quickly disappointed in the man for whom she had cut herself off from her own family, had been impatient with her elder daughter's lack of confidence, coupling it with her disability as a bar to matrimony. Reared in an atmosphere of censure, Helen had come to believe she was in truth inferior, and Vanessa did not delude herself into thinking that the task she had set herself would be an easy one.

She therefore waited for Helen to bring up the subject of Mr. Travers, which she did as they were making ready for bed, saying that she wondered if it was right for them to accept his generous invitation.

"If you are thinking it may be improper you are most probably right," Vanessa admitted, pinning a wayward ringlet firmly into place for the night. "But you must admit that it is a heaven-sent opportunity to find out if we are still able to ride. I've no mind to make a figure of myself by discovering in the middle of Brighton that I've lost the art! I can't think it would further our cause in the least." She tied an aged, frilled nightcap over her locks and paused consideringly. "Or would it be a good thing in your case? It might arouse a protective instinct!"

Helen laughed. "Vanessa, you are shocking!"

"I know, but one must consider these things from all angles! Are you worried in case we ought not to take advantage of Mr. Travers's good nature? Because if so, I can only say that he need not have made the offer and I believe it was genuinely meant. Not like Mrs. Ashley when we used to visit," she added, turning back the counterpane on the bed. "Always offering her carriage to take you home and plainly hoping you would refuse! Odious woman! No, I think Mr. Travers a very pleasant, agreeable gentleman, and I feel it would be churlish in us not to accept."

"I expect you are right," Helen said doubtfully. "But . . ."

"*But* you are being overscrupulous again! Of course, I know that under normal circumstances we would not go gallivanting around the countryside with a man to whom we have not been introduced and of whom we actually know nothing, but we could not possibly treat him to a distant bow after all his kindness when you were taken ill! We are so much beholden to him that if he wished for a little of our company in return I should feel obliged to give it even if I had taken a dislike to him. Which is not the case," she said, plumping up her pillows as she spoke to give her words a casual air. "I must confess that I am developing quite a partiality for him, and after all, where is the harm? I am sure he is completely trustworthy. Don't you like him also?"

Helen said quickly, "Indeed I do. We have met so few gentlemen that we cannot form comparisons, but I am sure that nowhere could be have met with more kindness and consideration."

Satisfied, Vanessa settled for the night, but long after they had extinguished their candles, she lay awake formulating plans for Mr. Travers's future, that would, to say the least, have startled him.

Accordingly, when she received Lord Pendril's invitation the following morning, she recommended to

Helen that they should give their second-best bonnets an airing, and armed with parasols against the strong sun, went down to meet him in the coffee room, which was situated on the opposite side of the hall from the tap. It was from here that Lord Pendril almost immediately emerged, his previous brisk constitutional having engendered a thirst that only Roberts's best brown ale could slake. Apparently under the impression that this second outing was also for their benefit, the terriers came too and retreated with pitifully flattened ears when ordered back to their quarters behind the bar.

It was a spectacle to wring the heart, and Helen turned appealing eyes to Lord Pendril as they set out on their tour. "Could they not come with us?"

He brightened perceptibly. "If you don't mind, but the little beggars can be a nuisance! Attack every dog on the road! The thing is, they expect to come with me now, and Patty don't like 'em!"

"With some justification you must admit," Vanessa said drily.

Lord Pendril snorted. "Why she must needs bring that damned poodle . . . ! Not that I've got anything against them on the whole," he explained. "M'mother's got one, and bar taking a nip out of you every now and then, it's a decent enough little dog. Even that don't cause as much trouble as it used to now it's lost most of its teeth."

"How—how fortunate!" Helen said, endeavoring not to laugh. "But where is Miss Morgan this morning?"

"Patty? She only gets up in time for luncheon!" Feeling Vanessa's eyes on him, he added hastily, "Habit, from working late in the theatre, I daresay."

Politely, she agreed with him. Reared by a nanny

with the strictest principles, she knew she ought to consider his liaison with Patty reprehensible, but for the life of her she could not. Examining this, she reached the conclusion that it was because he was so likable and so cheerfully frank about his transgressions that not even the most innocent of country maidens could possibly be deceived in him.

She waited while he threw a stick for the terriers, then in pursuance of her aims, said, "Mr. Travers was out early this morning, I believe."

"Went off somewhere at the crack of dawn! Mind you," he added, wrestling with one of the terriers, who had decided it was more amusing to hang on to the other end of the stick than to give it up, "he's always been the same. Sort of fellow who doesn't need any sleep." Gazing down affectionately on his adversary in the tug-of-war, he said, "What do you suggest we should call these little fellows? Seems a shocking thing that they shouldn't have names."

Vanessa, who had already heard them called several things, refused to be deterred. "I'm afraid I have never been able to think of them." She paused as it was plain she was not going to receive his full attention until he had won his battle over the missile, then said, "You have known Mr. Travers for a long time?"

"Since we were at Harrow. Used to stay with each other during the holidays," he said unguardedly.

"Is your home near here? I recall Mr. Travers telling us he is familiar with the district because he used to stay here frequently with a friend from Harrow."

With the resolve to corner Mr. Travers at the first opportunity and discover what other little gems he had invented for his past, Lord Pendril made haste to repair his mistake. "No, no. That wasn't me! Mutual

friend of ours had got a place near here. I dropped in
there but he's away."

"The same friend Mr. Travers had been going to
stay with?" Vanessa inquired dulcetly.

Lord Pendril realized he had inadvertently got himself in deeper. Thoroughly harassed, he said, "Eh! Was
he? Oh, yes, of course. Shall we go down this lane?
Less chance of meeting any stray dogs!"

He turned off the post road with more speed than
courtesy, leaving Vanessa with the conviction that
matters were not as straightforward as he and Mr.
Travers would have them believe, though which one
was guilty of the deception she could not decide.

Pondering this, she walked on slowly. The terriers
had dived into the ditch bordering the lane, forcing
their way through the brambles and undergrowth as
they followed the various trails with eager snuffles,
encouraged by Lord Pendril's cries of "Rats! Go get
'em!" Swinging along to keep up with them, the pace
he set was too quick for Helen, and Vanessa called out
to him to wait. With a quick grimace of apology, he
halted, and having him once more within her grasp
she continued her probe. Concluding that tact and
roundabout means were merely time consuming, she
plunged in with the most important question.

Endeavoring to make her tone unconcerned, she
said, "Is Mr. Travers married?"

She felt a hot blush spread up to her temples as
soon as she had voiced the question, but Lord Pendril
was too relieved to have an uncomplicated issue to notice it.

"Quentin married? Good Lord, no!" he said emphat-
ically.

Her blush subsiding, Vanessa scrutinized him

closely, the very forcefulness of his reply arousing suspicion again. Was this a further prevarication? Or was Mr. Travers perhaps in the habit of dallying with personable young women, but averse to matrimony?

Sighing, she decided to let events take their course. If it turned out that her hopes were justified, then presumably Mr. Travers would reveal his circumstances of his own volition. In the meantime she must hope that Helen did not lose her heart to a man unworthy of her, but watching her she was persuaded that she was already a little in love. As she walked ahead with Lord Pendril the change in her manner from a few days ago was marked, and her laugh rang out in a way Vanessa had seldom heard before.

She had confessed to Lord Pendril that she had a dread of rats, alive or dead, so he obligingly called the terriers off from their hunt and was once more entertaining them by throwing the stick, a game in which Helen was also partaking. They were equally eager to pursue the stick whichever one threw it, but Vanessa noted that they invariably returned it to Lord Pendril's hand, an observation that she kept to herself when his lordship called on her to remark how quickly they had taken to her sister.

Lord Pendril gallantly hid his own sentiments in a like manner when the question of their names once more arose, and Helen, appealed to, suggested that the one with the brown marking in his eyebrow should be christened Patch.

Vanessa was at one with his lordship in her opinion of this rather mundane appellation, but he said at once, "A capital idea! Make sure we never get 'em mixed up! Now what shall we call the other?"

Recalling the expletives regularly hurled at them

from the kitchens, Vanessa firmly suppressed the first suggestion that came to mind, and tongue in cheek, said, "Peter."

This was too much for Lord Pendril. Casting an astute glance in her direction, he said confidentially, "To tell you the truth, my brother-in-law is called Peter and he's the biggest bore I ever crossed. Can't think what possessed my sister to marry him!"

While negative in itself, this was productive of the notion that the remaining terrier should be called after someone he held in affection, and Lord Pendril immediately thought of his friend Barnaby Smethurst, since, he informed them, he was also a little, short-legged fellow and full of pluck.

They naturally spent most of the time afterward in teaching Barnaby and Patch to answer to their names, and the walk passed without incident except for such small diversions as the terriers putting up a large ginger tomcat that they discovered sunning itself in the peace of its own front garden. It leaped for the safety of a nearby tree, where it clung, spitting and snarling, until its owner, armed with a broom, came out to drive them away. Sensibly deciding that the tom was out of their reach, the terriers fell instead on the broom, so that Lord Pendril, his usual charm of manner availing him nothing, was forced to fall back on the use of his title to save himself from a situation that threatened him with being the loser. The elderly dame had second thoughts on the advisability of breaking the stave of her broom over the head of a viscount. Vanessa and Helen felt they had had sufficient excitement for one morning, and both being warm and thirsty, elected to return to the Angel where Lord Pendril promised them a cooling glass of lemonade.

But here again the arrival of the terriers proved to be ill timed. In the entrance hall, Roberts had just concluded the bargaining for a large green parrot that he hoped would prove an attraction in the tap, and had set the cage on the floor while he counted the purchase money into the unsavory hand of the vendor. The bird, slowly climbing the bars of the cage to view his new surroundings with a critical and unwinking eye, was the first object to be sighted by the newly christened Barnaby and Patch, and after freezing for a moment in pure disbelief, they charged. With a squawk of indignation, the parrot fell to the bottom of his cage in a flurry of brilliant green feathers, and Roberts, righteously incensed, kicked them out of the front door again. Unruffled, they got to their feet and shook themselves, but Roberts found himself the recipient of accusing glares from both Helen and Lord Pendril.

Bending to console them, Helen said in tones that trembled, "That was completely unwarranted! People should not have dogs if they ill treat them!" and, unconscious of the astonishment produced by her attack, continued to fondle them and murmur endearments.

Vanessa was rendered speechless by this completely unprecedented militancy on the part of her gentle sister, Lord Pendril regarded her with approval, and Roberts, opening his mouth to point out the plight of their unfortunate victim, closed it again and picked up the cage. Ill humored and disenchanted, the parrot climbed back on its perch, and Roberts carried it into the back premises where it would be safe until he could have a hook fixed at a height above the terriers' reach.

Lord Pendril and the ladies meanwhile adjourned to the coffee room, and it was here that Mr. Travers found them, together with Patty, a short while afterward. Roberts had greeted the arrival of three extra horses with a marked lack of enthusiasm, pointing out that he now had Lord Pendril's team, Mr. Travers's pair, and three hacks, as well as the animals belonging to his other guests, and if he should find himself in the unfortunate position of having all his post-horses returned at once he would very likely be forced to stand them in the courtyard.

Mr. Travers merely grinned and told him he was expecting a package to be handed in, then prudently withdrew to his room to wash and scan through the newspapers until he judged Thomas to be well on his way back to the Court. When he descended to inquire for the parcel, Roberts produced it from behind the counter, muttering of the dire results of such perilous goings on. Mr. Travers took it with a slight feeling of relief. He had been unable to rid his mind of the suspicion that his sister intended to turn up with it in person, and had been vainly trying to concoat some story that would both satisfy the Misses Hartland and preserve the illusion he had created.

Bearing the parcel, and guided by Patty's carrying accents, he entered the coffee room and presented it to Vanessa.

"The last of our problems solved," he said. "A riding habit for you."

Surprised, she smiled up at him. "However did you manage to obtain one so quickly?"

"It was lent to me by the sister of the friend I told you of," he replied, offering up a small prayer that no one would tell her the actual time of his return or she would think the fictional friend's sister rose at a very odd hour in the morning. He became aware that Lord Pendril was watching him with an anguished expression and correctly divined that his lordship had met with some difficulties in his absence.

Feeling his way, he said, "I borrowed some horses from George Harmer up at the Court, and Miss Caroline most kindly provided the loan of a habit."

Vanessa said she must write a note to thank her, and Lord Pendril, who had always understood that George Harmer's family seat was in Essex, accepted his transportation without a blink. Exerting a warning pressure on Patty's foot, he said, "Very obliging girl, Miss Caroline. Queer thing that you and I should both have happened to call on George at about the same time!"

"A remarkable coincidence," Mr. Travers agreed. "But I count myself fortunate in his absence." He bowed to Vanessa and Helen. "I should otherwise have missed some very delightful company."

Bent on revenge for the unease he had suffered on Mr. Travers's behalf, Lord Pendril said, "I expect now that you'll all be going out this afternoon, so I think I'll take Patty into Daventry in the curricle. Beats me how she could have forgotten anything with all we had strapped up behind, but that's women for you. She's got to do some shopping."

Patty regarded him indulgently. "Bess packed in a hurry."

"Not so much of a hurry that you forgot him!" Lord

Pendril said, bestowing a sour glance on Jason. "I suppose he'll be coming with us!"

Patty gave him to understand that he was correct in this, and having appropriated Mr. Travers's curricle and pair, Lord Pendril prudently decided to depart before he had an opportunity to object to such blatant piracy. He shepherded Patty out to the accompaniment of Mr. Traver's murmured, "I'll serve you out for that one day!" and with no more delay than it took to have the bays harnessed and for Patty to twice change her outfit, they were on the road to Daventry.

Here Lord Pendril spent a trying afternoon following her about and objecting to her expenditure. He had left the bays at an inn, and Patty casually loaded her purchases on to him until he protested that he felt like a damned footman. Complaining at length, he carried them back to the inn where he found that Patty expected him to buy her tea to sustain her on the return journey. She supplemented this beverage with a variety of sweet cakes without inciting him to more than a sneer, but when she ordered a beefsteak to be minced fine and served in a bowl to Jason, his command slipped and he so far forgot himself as to voice his opinion of what would be a more suitable repast.

At the height of the ensuing disagreement, Patty stormed out to the curricle, and Lord Pendril, becoming profane, seized on a waiter conveniently by and ordered him to carry her parcels after her. He was piling these about her feet with a total disregard for her comfort when a barouche drew up alongside, and a voice that above all others he found least welcome said:

"Charles!"

An unpleasant sensation coursing up his spine, Lord

Pendril straightened to meet the steely gaze transfixing him.

"Charles!" repeated Mrs. Travers, with all the authority of one who had known him from a schoolboy. *"Where is Quentin?"*

Chapter Four

"No word of a lie, dear boy," Lord Pendril said. "Gave me the worst turn I've ever had! I could have got out of it easily enough in the normal way, but she'd recognized those bays!"

"What did you say?" Mr. Travers asked. He had returned from a most successful outing, in the course of which, without undue conceit, he felt he had considerably advanced his cause, to be met by the intelligence that Lord Pendril wished to see him without a second's delay.

"Told her I'd bought them off you of course! What else could I say? Mind you," he went on gloomily, "she didn't believe me, as you might know. Right there, in front of your sister and Patty, not to mention the waiter and every fool on the street, she said she'd thank me not to prevaricate on your behalf and demanded to know where you were! I told her I didn't know and I hadn't seen you, but she only said she hoped I was ashamed of myself. I felt about fifteen again, I can tell you!"

"You didn't tell her where you were staying?" Mr. Travers said.

Lord Pendril gave him a pained look. "I can't remember the half of what I said, but my wits weren't that far gone! She thinks I was putting up in Daventry, so with a bit of luck she'll search there first, but what happens when she gets home? She'll start on your groom and then she'll know for certain that you haven't sold the bays!"

"And that I've sent for the hacks!" Mr. Travers said, getting to his feet. "I'd better get poor Walker out of there or she'll annihilate him!"

"You'll end up with your entire staff lodged at the Angel," Lord Pendril told him. "I hope you find it's worth it!"

"So do I," Mr. Travers said, somewhat ruefully. "Did you say Caroline was with my stepmother?" As Lord Pendril nodded, he said, "Hm," and disappeared to find Roberts.

As a result of his activities, Walker arrived at the Angel two hours later. He had with him only the minimum of clothing and he was forced to share an attic room with the Angel's head groom, the hostelry being as full as it could hold, but he felt these evils were outweighed by the facts that he now had the bays under his personal supervision again and there was no longer the prospect that he might be called upon to face Mrs. Travers.

Patty also was restored to high good humor by the spectacle of Lord Pendril being severely trounced in the high street of Daventry; and Vanessa and Helen, though suffering from expected stiffness, were cheered to discover that their equestrian ability had not entirely deserted them. In addition, Vanessa was elated by a further confirmation of her hopes with regard to Helen. It had not occurred to Mr. Travers until the horses were being led into the courtyard that he did not know the reason for Helen's lameness and he could conceivably be causing harm by his well-meant suggestion. Suddenly concerned, he drew Vanessa to one side for a low-voiced question, and she could not mistake his sincerity.

She reassured him that Helen was not suffering from any physical weakness; as a child, for some reason that the doctors could not explain, the growth of one leg had failed to keep pace with the other, but she had never suffered any pain or instability as a result of it, and Vanessa had no fear that there was the slightest risk of injury.

Mr. Travers, therefore, exerted himself to please. He was by far too courteous and well bred to show a preference for Vanessa when he had invited them both, and constituting himself instructor, he soon found Helen needed more of his attention. By nature she was not as capable as Vanessa, so that he found himself more often at her side, advising and correcting and gently encouraging her to exert her authority. All told, it was a pleasant afternoon. The weather was hot but not oppressively so, and bearing in mind that his horses, with the feel of turf under their hooves, might be tempted to go faster than their riders were ready for, he took them through woods and a series of quiet lanes where they met little traffic. Both retained a good deal of their original experience so that they were not obliged to exert all their energies on the awkward business of not falling off, and at the end of the ride Mr. Travers was able to compliment them on their rapid progress.

Vanessa said lightheartedly that it was a great comfort to know they had not made an exhibition of themselves, but later, when Helen was out of earshot, she tried to tell him of her genuine gratitude.

Uncomfortably aware that his motives were by no means as pure as she believed, Mr. Travers dismissed her thanks, but since this was productive of another glowing look, his conscience prompted him to remove himself before she could embarrass him further.

It was at this juncture that Lord Pendril informed him of his possibly imminent discovery by his stepmother, and an unnatural recklessness was born in him. If tomorrow should determine that he was revealed in all his wealth, then he wished to know tonight whether the ordinary Mr. Travers had the power to oust the vision of the affluent merchant from Vanessa's ambitious thoughts.

Voicing his intention to Lord Pendril, he was met by a blank stare. When he had recovered his powers of speech, his lordship said, "You're never going to propose to a girl you've only known two days!"

"No, no," Mr. Travers murmured. "I must confess that, along with Miss Hartland I have no doubt, I should be wary of committing myself for life on so short an acquaintance."

"What are you going to do then?" Lord Pendril demanded. "Ask her if she thinks she might like to marry you when she gets to know you better?"

But this Mr. Travers was not inclined to answer. For one thing, he had no very clear idea himself, but he had confidence in his own resourcefulness and he did not doubt that before the evening was out, he would have ascertained, if not the complete answer, at least enough on which to form a later judgment.

They gathered together in the private parlor in time for dinner and nothing occurred to mar the evening. Patty, with rare consideration, had Bess take Jason for a walk and then keep him in the bedroom so that Lord Pendril was not disturbed by his company, and in response, Lord Pendril kindly refrained from abusing him in his absence. Roberts's wife had surpassed herself both in the cooking and the presentation of the meal, and it was while they were deciding between the broiled chickens, loin of roast mutton, and a dish of partridges, which formed the main dishes of the second course, that Patty discovered that Helen and Vanessa had never been to a play. During the rest of the meal, she entertained them with tales from the theatre that were not only guaranteed to destroy all their illusions at any future performance they might witness, but that would have been considered highly slanderous by many leading actors of the day.

Since Mr. Travers and Lord Pendril pronounced the Burgundy excellent, Patty then took a couple of glasses to confirm their opinion and embarked on some of her favorite stage roles. She was principally a comedy actress and the reactions of even such a limited audience soon brought Roberts in to find out what was causing so much merriment. He came ostensibly to offer a claret that he thought might appeal more to the taste of the ladies, and was only driven out again when Vanessa exacerbated his sensibilities by adding water to hers. She was aware that by this act she had also incurred the disapproval of Mr. Travers and Lord Pendril, but laughter and the lingering heat of the day, together with the wine during dinner, had rendered her cheeks warm and she feared they might begin to flush unbecomingly.

The truth was that she could not recall enjoying an evening so much in her life before. The last year they had been in mourning, and the previous eighteen months had been shadowed by their mother's illness. The few occasions when they had been able to accept invitations, the company had all been of their mother's generation or older, and mostly of a sober and excessively respectable turn of mind. Patty, she knew, would have been totally disapproved of by all of them from the squire's wife downward, and Lord Pendril was undoubtedly what she had heard referred to in hushed tones as a rake. She could imagine their lips folding tightly if they could see her now and wondered briefly if her present enjoyment had betrayed her into a want of conduct. Catching Mr. Travers's eye, she was reassured when he smiled at her warmly. Mr. Travers was most truly the gentleman and she felt instinctively that he would check her if she went beyond what was permissible. Mr. Travers, in fact, was all that she had ever hoped for or imagined when she had envisaged Helen's future.

Patty came to the end of her repertoire amidst a burst of applause that interrupted Vanessa's thoughts. Helen was begging her to continue, but Patty shook her head vigorously and leaned back, fanning herself. "Must think of my voice. I've done more tonight than I would in a complete performance! It's not every day I play four parts!"

Lord Pendril immediately passed her a glass of wine to soothe her throat and suggested that she should give them a ballet to round it off. Rapping him sharply over the knuckles, Patty told him to behave himself. "No, what we need now is a quiet game of cards, though five's an awkward number."

"Whist," Lord Pendril said with a grin. "And the odd one out can play solitaire!"

"Not," Mr. Travers told him, "unless you have the intention of sitting out yourself! I'm not in the mood for being fleeced tonight." Lord Pendril grinned again, and Mr. Travers said, "Let me warn you, ladies, never to indulge in anything more serious than a game of speculation with Charles! He thought at one time to maintain himself on the proceeds of whist and piquet, but the number of his friends who can be persuaded to sit down to a table with him is rapidly diminishing, and is now composed either of those who are to timid to refuse a challenge or the unfortunates who have never played against him before and are unaware of their risk!"

Lord Pendril protested, and Vanessa looked at him reproachfully. "Say no more! Speculation it shall be!"

His lordship's jaw dropped in dismay, but his early upbringing came to his rescue, and ten minutes later, his mother, could she have been there, would have been gladdened by the sight of her eldest son joining in a pastime that he had avoided since his youth. Patty also declared that she hadn't played since she didn't know when, and possibly because it was a game prevailing more in the less sophisticated society to which they had been accustomed, Vanessa and Helen finished the evening modest winners.

Sorting Vanessa's coins into neat piles, Mr. Travers said, "In addition to not playing whist with Charles, remind me never again to take on the Misses Hartland in speculation. It is a course that can only lead to ruin!"

Vanessa chuckled. "Are you quite done up, sir?"

"Oh, completely! How about you, Charles?"

Lord Pendril solemnly turned out his pockets. "Finished!" he said. "What with that and a shocking bonnet Patty bought this afternoon in Daventry! Daventry!" he repeated accusingly. "And if I know anything of it she'll never put it on her head when she gets to London! I'll take a bet here and now that she'll have given it to Bess inside a month!"

Aware that this would most likely prove to be true, Patty said hurriedly that she was going to retire, and Lord Pendril, his sense of propriety dimmed by Burgundy, patted her ample rear proportions in a gesture of farewell.

Tactfully averting their eyes, Vanessa and Helen rose to their feet also, and Mr. Travers realized that the evening had gone by and he was no nearer the answer to his most pressing question. He directed a meaningful glance at Lord Pendril that earned him a look of startled query in return, but his lordship, deducing from Mr. Travers's infinitesimal nod that he had judged the message correctly, obediently engaged Vanessa in conversation and drifted toward the hall. When Helen made to follow them, Mr. Travers detained her with a hand on her arm and partially closed the door.

Meeting her surprised gaze, he smiled. "Forgive me, Miss Helen, but I wished to have a word with you on a subject of great delicacy." He paused, wondering how to phrase the question, and said finally, "You are perhaps aware that I have a great . . . admiration for your sister. I know this is a subject on which I have no right to speak to you, and in the ordinary way I should not do so, but there are circumstances . . ." He halted again and she continued to regard him steadily. "Miss

Helen, you comprehend my meaning, I am sure, and if you feel unable to give me an answer I shall perfectly understand. I am not asking you to betray a confidence, but if you could give me only a hint?"

She remained silent for a moment, her eyes lowered, and they heard Vanessa call her name from the hall. He reached out to take her hand, saying, "Quickly, in case she returns!"

She raised her eyes to his. "Sir, I cannot answer your question properly, for in truth I do not know, but I will tell you that from small things she has said, I believe her to be . . . not indifferent to your regard."

He released her hand and, stepping back, said, "Thank you! That is all I wished to know. You will say nothing to her of this?"

She shook her head, and at that moment Vanessa pushed open the door of the parlor. "Helen, are . . . ?" She broke off, seeing that Helen looked flustered. "Are you coming?"

"I was just going to." She smiled at Mr. Travers. "Good night, sir."

"Good night, Miss Helen, Miss Vanessa!" With a small bow, he held back the door for them and in thoughtful silence they made their way up to their room.

They were much later going to bed than they were accustomed to, and by tacit agreement blew out their candles without sitting up to read for a while as they normally did. But in spite of a pleasant tiredness, sleep eluded Vanessa. Lying in the darkness, her eyes fixed on the square of moonlit sky outside the window, she dwelt on the little scene she had witnessed, her mind turning over its implications.

Finally, she said cautiously, "Helen? Are you awake?"

At once Helen eased herslf up in the bed. "Yes. I was trying to lie still because I thought you were asleep and I was afraid of disturbing you."

Vanessa chuckled. "So was I." Turning her head, she said, "Was Mr. Travers talking of anything in particular when I came in?"

There was not enough light for her to distinguish Helen's face, but she could hear the smile in her voice as she replied, "Yes, but you needn't tease me to tell you what it was, for I shan't."

Coaxingly, Vanessa said, "If it was something pleasant . . ."

"Very pleasant!"

"Then why can't you tell me?"

But Helen would only shake her head in the darkness, and Vanessa was forced to be content with her surmise.

They did not see Mr. Travers and Lord Pendril when they went down to breakfast, as the two gentlemen had arranged to take their rods down to the river. In their absence they would not take advantage of the private parlor, though Roberts obviously expected them to do so, but led the way firmly into the public dining room. Here they were immediately made aware of the preferential treatment they had formerly received. The room was crowded. Apart from the residents of the inn, a great many travelers seemed to have stopped for their first meal, including a rather noisy party of young men who broke off an argument to stare at them as they went by. It was plain from their accents and dress that they were of unexceptionable background, and while their gaze betokened nothing more than appreciation, Vanessa could not be comfortable, and seated herself and Helen as far away from them as possible.

This brought them into closer proximity with Mrs. Moorcroft and her companion than Vanessa would have chosen, but since they were only treated to a cold nod by the former, it seemed unlikely that they would be drawn into any unwelcome conversation. But as Vanessa concentrated on trying to catch the eye of the overburdened serving man she could not avoid hearing part of what was said, and unmistakably the subject of their discussion was Patty. During the interval between ordering and receiving their coffee she learned that Mrs. Moorcroft considered it disgusting that respectable women should be forced to share the same roof as creatures of her moral character, and that she was convinced that the hussy was an actress. Remembering Patty's performance of the previous evening, Vanessa was unable to repress a smile. It was intended only for Helen, but unfortunately Mrs. Moorcroft observed it and seemed to take it as a personal affront and the confirmation of her belief that willing associates of such a female must themselves be beyond recall.

To let them know the depths to which they had sunk she began a similar condemnation of Lord Pendril's conduct, but since they had heard it all before, Helen and Vanessa continued to sip their coffee unmoved. It was not until she leaned forward and said, "And that Mr. Travers too!" that Vanessa experienced anything other than amusement. But the last disclosure was a shock. While she was telling herself that she could easily have misunderstood the significance of the remark, Mrs. Moorcroft repeated how she had with her own eyes seen Mr. Travers leaving Patty's room, thus dispelling the possibility of mistake. Hoping her face did not betray her, she calmly refilled her cup and by an effort of will prevented herself from looking in their direction. But though she could not see it, her mind all too clearly pictured Mrs. Moorcroft's expression of avid interest, and she no longer had any appetite for the food the waiter was placing before them.

Glancing up quickly, she saw distress mirrored in Helen's eyes, and raged inwardly. Mr. Travers had caused her sister to suffer pain and he would not lightly be forgiven. She forced herself to carry on with her breakfast, but she was thankful when it was finished and they could leave. Perversity made her bestow a smiling "Good morning" on the two as she passed, and she had the satisfaction of seeing Mrs. Moorcroft's face twitch in surprise, but once outside her tongue seemed to freeze in her mouth and she could neither utter condemnation nor comfort.

It was Helen who first spoke. Calmly, she said, "We know Mr. Travers to have a great many good qualities, and I think perhaps we ought not to place too much dependence on what was said. Also . . ." she paused, and then went on with heightened color. "Also, we have been so restricted . . . It may be that we are placing too great an importance on something that is perhaps not regarded nearly so seriously by . . . by more worldly people."

"You mean we're country bumpkins!" Vanessa said flatly.

Helen nodded and Vanessa silently considered this. For herself, she did not think she could ever countenance any division in the attentions of a man she loved, but she had no right to make arbitrary decisions on her sister's behalf. If Helen's feelings were different from her own, she could be at fault in trying to influence her.

She said, "Then we will let Mr. Travers's actions toward us be our guide and forget all about Mrs. Moorcroft! Shall we go for a walk? It seems a pity to be indoors on such a beautiful day."

Helen acquiesced and they went upstairs for their bonnets and parasols. On returning to the hall they were met by Barnaby and Patch, who expressed their willingness to accompany them, but their offer was firmly declined by Vanessa who felt herself unequal to dealing with stray dogs and the owners of any cats they might meet on their route. The terriers, however, were not to be turned down so easily, and in the end the ladies were forced to ask Roberts to shut them up in the rear quarters so that they could make their escape. Helen lamented the necessity for this, and Roberts was privately concerned for the safety of his parrot, though it was by no means the wonderful talker he had been led to believe. Such few words as it uttered were so indistinct that even if its language was doubtful it could not give offense, so to please his wife, who declared she could not abide its nasty cold eye watching her around the room all the time, and to avoid needless confrontation with the terriers, he hung its cage from a suitably high beam in the coffee room.

Helen and Vanessa meanwhile, followed the way down to the river that Mr. Travers had taken Vanessa on the first morning, but, with no vision of intent anglers rewarding their gaze, they strolled through the fields toward the village green. This was a large triangle of grass in the center of the village. It had a small stream and pond and was pleasantly shaded by trees, which made it the place for all the village women to meet and gossip and the young girls to accidentally encounter the unmarried young men. They had walked around it the previous day with Lord Pendril and Vanessa had been amused by the sidelong glances cast on these carefully contrived meetings. But when they arrived on this occasion it was to find a band of gypsies and caravan dwellers encamped at one end, and, viewing the assortment of whippets and mongrels, Vanessa was thankful that Barnaby and Patch were safely shut up at the inn. Children and dogs fought between the hobbled ponies and a troupe of jugglers practiced in a clearing between the caravans. Vanessa would have been interested to watch if they had not been alone, but bearing the terrible stories told by their nanny of the gypsies' wicked ways, they skirted the encampment widely and returned to the Angel.

Here, Helen's first concern was to make sure the terriers had been released. Rendered intrepid by her interest in their welfare, she braved the depths at the back of the inn while Vanessa slowly climbed the stairs, loitering so that her sister might catch up with her. When she was halfway up and level with the taproom, she heard Lord Pendril and Mr. Travers enter it by the street entrance, but since ladies did not commonly go into the tap, she merely paused to see if they would come out. Their attention, however, was immediately claimed by Roberts.

His voice urgent, he said, "Mr. Travers! Your ma-in-law was in here not half an hour since!"

Sharply, Mr. Travers said, "What? You didn't tell her I was staying here?"

"I said you had been, you'd paid your shot and left this morning early. I daren't say I hadn't seen you in case she was to question the servants. I've warned them all now in case she comes back, which it's my belief she will. I did my best, but I can't say she seemed satisfied!"

"Devil take her!" Mr. Travers said with feeling. "All I needed was a few more days!"

On the stairs, Vanessa grasped the bannisters with fingers gone suddenly nerveless. If Mr. Travers had a mother-in-law then he must have a wife! And for what did he need only a few more days?

Disastrously clear came Lord Pendril's gloomy, "That's played out your little game, Quentin, my boy! No point in staying here now. When she comes back she'd find me as well, which I'll admit I'd sooner she didn't!"

What Mr. Travers replied, Vanessa did not hear. Picking up her skirts she flew up the stairs to the half landing. Here, the sound of a door opening made her shrink back against the wall, but it was not the door of the tap but the front door. A very pretty young brunette came through and paused just inside, her wide gray eyes looking around inquiringly. She was a complete stranger; and disinterested and numbed by what she had overheard, Vanessa was just about to turn away when the girl's face changed, and an expression half fearful, half appealing came over it.

Starting forward, she said, "Quentin!" and as he came up to her, she stood on tiptoe to kiss his cheek. Mr. Travers submitted to the embrace, but the absence of welcome was marked.

"I might have known you would be here as well!" he said resignedly.

Chapter Five

In her bedroom, Vanessa leaned her head against the door for a moment. The sense of physical shock at first seemed to slow down her mind so that thoughts would not come, then with a desperate urgency she began to snatch her clothes from the drawers and throw them on the bed. When Helen arrived they were piled in an untidy heap, but intent on disentangling the fringe of her shawl, she did not immediately perceive them. Her eyes fixed on her task as she delicately unpicked a knot, she said, "I have just seen Lord Pendril and Mr. Travers in the coffee room with the prettiest girl! I wonder who she could be? They did not see me as I went by, so I . . ." She broke off to stare as Vanessa crossed the room with another armful of clothes and dropped them on the counterpane. "Vanessa! What is the matter? What are you doing?"

"Packing!" Vanessa said. She sat down suddenly on the bed. "Helen, we must leave here at once! I have just made the most dreadful discovery! I—I hardly know how to say it, but—but Mr. Travers is married!"

The last words came out with a rush, and Helen's hand flew to her cheek. "Married?" she repeated stupidly. "No, he cannot be, not after what—Vanessa, there must be some mistake!"

Vanessa shook her head. "No." She looked up and met Helen's eyes, reading the bewilderment and hurt in them. "That girl downstairs—you saw them together—did nothing strike you in his manner?"

Slowly, Helen said, "I did not like to mention it, but yes. As I said, they did not see me go by, and when I was coming up the stairs Mr. Travers closed the door quickly, as though he did not wish them to be observed. Are you saying . . . ? Do you think she is . . . ?" She stopped, unable to finish the sentence, and Vanessa nodded again.

"Yes, I believe she must be his wife!" She crossed the room once more and flung out the shoes and oddments from the bottom of the wardrobe. "If we leave at once we may be able to avoid meeting him again! We owe him a certain civility for his help when we arrived here, but if we came face to face with him, I don't think I *could* be civil! If we pack now, we can hire a chaise to take us into Daventry and catch the Mail from there tomorrow." She had been dragging the trunk into the middle of the room as she spoke, but halfway her voice trembled and she sat back on her heels. Her eyes filling with tears, Helen ran to kneel beside her, then Vanessa blew her nose and achieved a watery smile.

"Well, I suppose it is quite our own fault for being gullible. I hold myself to blame because I knew all along that there was a—a want of openness in Mr.

Travers, but I chose to ignore it. At least we shall
know better than to be so foolish another time! It
must be a lesson to us never again to indulge our
fancy with anyone who has not been properly presented to us!" She added unconvincingly, "I daresay
we shall have forgotten all about Mr. Travers in a
week or two!"

"Yes," Helen agreed. She tried to match Vanessa's
valiant tone, but the tears started to her eyes again
and she turned her head to wipe them away. "I wonder why Mr. Travers concealed that he was married? I
cannot see the reason for such a pretense!"

Vanessa remembered his words: "*All I needed was
a few more days.*" She could not bring herself to repeat them to Helen, but her sister must learn the
truth. Bluntly, she said, "Since we have learned that
he makes a practice of visiting Miss Morgan even in
this inn, I don't think we have far to search for the
reason!" She saw Helen's eyes widen in horror, and
smiled wryly. "Though in any case he was doomed to
disappoint on such a count! He thought he had found
himself an ignorant country girl, but he would very
soon learn that our principles are higher in the country!"

She applied herself to her packing again, but Helen
still stood where she was. "Vanessa, he cannot have
believed . . . Are you positive there can be no mistake?"

"Positive!" Vanessa said vehemently. She realized
she had not told Helen how she had made the discovery, and paused, her hands resting on the trunk. "I
was on the stairs when Mr. Travers and Lord Pendril
went into the taproom. Roberts, from the way he
spoke, had been waiting for them to come in, and Mr.

Travers was barely through the door before he told him his mother-in-law had been here looking for him! Roberts had fobbed her off, but he was warning Mr. Travers because he thought she might come back. They were all very concerned, and Lord Pendril said, 'That's played out your little game!' and something about there being no point in them staying now. Oh, I cannot remember the exact words, but there was no mistaking the meaning! If you had been there you would know! And then that girl came in through the front and went up to Mr. Travers and kissed him! So," she concluded, pushing her dresses down viciously into the trunk, "unless he is on terms of such familiarity with any number of young women, I think we may presume she is his wife. It must be highly inconvenient for him to have her turn up like that, and certainly he was not in the least pleased to see her, poor thing! I daresay, between them, they have hustled her away again by now!"

"Then Lord Pendril was a party to it," Helen said sadly.

"Of course he was! If he and Mr. Travers are such old friends he must know very well that he is married! The two of them have duped us finely!"

Helen made no reply. She could only be thankful that Vanessa did not know the content of Mr. Travers's conversation with her the previous evening, or the blow would have been doubly hard. Silently she began to fold her own dresses to go with Vanessa's, and soon the only signs of their occupation in the room were their redingotes hanging over the back of the chair, and the open trunk. As she put the medicines in the top and closed the lid, Vanessa said, "And don't you dare give me cause to get these out again!"

Helen smiled wanly. "I shan't, I promise you. I cannot be comfortable until we are away from here, though I am sorry to—to be leaving those dear little dogs." She ducked her head to hide renewed tears, and Vanessa looked up, her expression softening. "You shall have two just like them as soon as we are settled in Brighton." She finished cording the trunk and got to her feet. "It is time to pay our bill. Shall you want any luncheon before we leave?"

Helen shook her head, and in spite of having had little breakfast, Vanessa knew she could not eat anything. With only their luggage to be carried down there was nothing to delay them longer in the bedchamber, so they went to bespeak the chaise and pay what was owed for their stay. Roberts's face was a picture of astonishment when it was revealed that they wished to leave at once, and to avoid the questions hovering on his lips as well as the possible mischance of a meeting with Mr. Travers, Vanessa ordered lemonade to be sent to them in the coffee room while they were waiting for the chaise to be brought around to the front. Here she stood by the window, nervously scanning the road for the vehicle to appear and dreading every moment to hear Mr. Travers's voice outside the door. She suspected that Roberts would lose no time in informing him of their strange action and several times she exclaimed restlessly, "Oh, what can be keeping them so long!"

The question was rhetorical and Helen only shook her head. In contrast to her sister's pacing, she sat at the table in a listless attitude, smiling occasionally at the parrot, who was turning stately somersaults on the bars of his cage to attract her attention. There were only the two of them in the room, but such was Vanessa's concentration on the road outside that it was several minutes before she noticed the sound she had come to dread. Turning sharply, her worst fears were realized. Helen was leaning back, her fingers gripping the edge of the table, and the rasp in her lungs increasing with every breath she drew.

For a moment, Vanessa stood frozen. Her first thought was that now they would not be able to leave, but hard on it was the realization that never before had an attack come on Helen with such appalling suddenness. Already the strength seemed to be draining from her and the noise of her breathing filled the room.

Pushing back a feeling of panic, Vanessa ran across to her, and half dragging, half supporting her, managed to get her to the chintz-covered window seat. Raising her legs, she laid her back on it, and after thrusting cushions under her head and shoulders, tugged violently on the bell to summon Roberts.

It seemed an agonizing age before he came, and Helen worsened by the minute. Her fight for breath was terrifying to watch and Vanessa flung all the casements open in a desperate attempt to get more air into the room. By the time Roberts arrived she was sobbing with fright and barely able to get her words out. Fortunately, he needed no telling. Remembering the conditions under which she had arrived at the Angel in the first instance, he shouted to his wife to bring hot water, dispatched the tapster and two of the serving men to scour the village until they found the doctor, and carried the trunk into the coffee room. He cut through the knots to get it open more quickly, and when his wife hastened in with the hot water, snatched the apron from about her waist to drape around Helen's head. As they waited in a tense semi-circle listening to the harsh sound of her breathing, it seemed, though none of them would voice the hope, that it gradually eased. There was nothing more they could do, and Mrs. Roberts, after a glance at Vanessa's strained white face, told her husband to hold the bowl, and fetched a glass of brandy. This, in spite of her protests, she obliged Vanessa to drink, and by the time the doctor arrived she was tolerably composed.

By good fortune he had been in when the messenger called at his house and the intelligence that the patient was a friend of Mr. Travers had brought him out at once. An experienced, practical man, he asked few questions until he had examined Helen, then ordered her to be carried up to the bedchamber again. Only when Vanessa and Mrs. Roberts had undressed her and got her between the sheets did he check on the medicines and inquire from Vanessa what had led up to the attack. This he did minutely, carefully taking down the frequency and severity of Helen's previous illnesses, and reading and rereading his notes with an expression it was impossible to fathom.

Finally, he looked up from his papers and smiled at Vanessa. "Well, young lady, I will relieve your anxiety! I can assure you that your sister will recover, and probably quite quickly!"

Vanessa could only whisper, "Thank you!" Her former terror had given way to a quiet desperation. When they left their home she had made her plans for the future so blithely, confident that she could cope with anything, but as she sat and watched Helen it had seemed that if she lived, it would take a miracle to complete their journey. Glancing toward the bed, she said in a low voice, "I have noticed that she is always more prone to these when she is disturbed for some reason, but she has never been so bad before! Do you think it was the prospect of traveling that caused it?"

"I have come across cases where emotional upset would bring on such an attack. As for the travel, a few drops of laudanum to bring about a calming effect may be helpful, though I do not advise its indiscriminate use." He paused, smiling again. "But as regards her present illness, you may take that troubled expression off your face, for no, it was not caused by the prospect of travel, nor will you be obliged to spend the rest of your lives at this admittedly excellent hostelry! For the future, Miss Hartland, I would advise you never to allow your sister to sit in the same room as a parrot!"

"A parrot!" Vanessa exclaimed.

"Or a canary or any other bird! Your sister, my dear, in common with another of my patients, is adversely affected by them! Let me say that it is only my own observation, but I have no doubt of it being the cause in this case."

"Oh, thank heavens!" Vanessa said. "We are on our way to Brighton, and it may seem foolish, but I was beginning to think we should be forced to walk if we were ever to reach there!"

"Then I am glad to be able to set your mind at rest. For the moment your sister should remain quietly in bed but she may get up as soon as she feels well enough. Take care and use common sense. I cannot improve on her medicines so you will continue to treat her as you have done in the past." Rising to his feet, he collected up his notes and put them in the pocket of his frock coat. "Call on me again if you are worried, though I do not anticipate that it will be necessary."

Vanessa thanked him, and after paying his discreetly mentioned bill, escorted him out. The fee was money they could ill afford, but she felt it was worth every penny for the tremendous relief his words had brought her. It was not until she had checked on Helen and was sitting quietly by the window with a book that it occurred to her again that they would now be unable to avoid a further meeting with Mr. Travers. If Roberts had already told him that she and Helen had been on the point of leaving, their next encounter would be greatly embarrassing. She sat rehearsing several excuses, all of them feeble. It was impossible to give him the true reason, for that was to betray the hopes she had nursed, and she would rather face death than Mr. Travers's amused expression were he ever to learn of them. Nor could she accuse him of having deceived them, for in actual fact he had not done so. Lord Pendril had certainly denied that he was married, whether on Mr. Travers's instructions or not she could not know, but Mr. Travers himself had only by omission led them to believe he was a bachelor. He could easily excuse himself in the whole affair on the grounds that she had come to a false conclusion and misread a few acts of kindness. At the end of twenty minutes this thought had taken such a strong hold on her that she began to wonder if this was not indeed the case. Setting out in her mind, incident by incident, the small things that had seemed to argue a particular interest in Helen, she found on examination that they were insubstantial. Mr. Travers could hardly be held responsible if a silly inexperienced girl misinterpreted his actions. Even the damning conversation she had overheard no longer seemed so sinister. Would she have come to the same conclusion without Mrs. Moorcroft's spiteful piece of information? It was hard to imagine what else the words could mean, but she had to admit that she had given Mr. Travers no opportunity to explain them.

Her mind running on, she visualized a confrontation with him, and herself saying, "You have deceived us, Mr. Travers! We had no idea you were married!" and Mr. Travers, with a lift to his brows, replying, "Did I not mention it? But how have I deceived you?"

The picture made her cheeks burn hotly, and she wished with all her heart that they were safe in Daventry. In all probability he would come up to inquire about Helen as soon as he learned what had happened, and he would certainly also ask why they had been fleeing the Angel without even the conventional farewell that good manners demanded. The only possible escape was to ask Roberts, if he had not already told him, not to mention their intended departure. She shrank inwardly from the thought, but it was better than the alternative. If she was going to do it there was no time to be lost, so she told Helen she was going downstairs for a few minutes, took a deep breath, and resolutely descended to the hall. Roberts was nowhere to be seen and in the interval it took a serving maid to find him her courage almost deserted her. She managed to reply coherently when he asked after Helen, but an obstacle seemed to rise in her throat when it came to the reason for wishing to see him.

The silence lengthened, and finally she blurted out, "Did you . . . Is Mr. Travers aware that we intended leaving this morning?"

His face carefully inscrutable, Roberts said he had

not seen Mr. Travers since he came in from his fishing.

Quite faint with relief, Vanessa said, "Then I should be very much obliged if you would not tell him." She tried to think of some valid reason for such an extraordinary request but none presented itself. "We have changed our minds and we shall be staying a few more days, and—well, I should be grateful if you would not mention it."

Roberts said, "Not if you don't wish it, ma'am," and she nodded her thanks and made her exit with as much dignity as she could muster.

The precarious comfort this interview afforded her would have been shattered could she have overheard Roberts a short while afterward. Not unduly chivalrous at his best, he rated Mr. Travers's interests very much higher than Vanessa's, and without the smallest compunction immediately went in search of him. Discovering him eventually in Lord Pendril's room, he repeated the gist of the conversation together with the rest of the day's events. He was heard out in silence, Mr. Travers merely remarking, "Curious!" when he came to the end of his narration.

"Curious!" Lord Pendril exclaimed. "It's downright queer! What's more, it's dashed bad manners! Ask her what she meant by it!"

"I can't," Mr. Travers pointed out. "Roberts says he promised not to tell us!"

Lord Pendril considered the ethics of this for a moment, then said reluctantly, "I suppose not, but by God, if it was me I'd want to know the reason!"

"I do want to know it! Let us consider the facts of the matter as they occur. There was certainly no suggestion of this last night, so it is therefore some-

thing that had happened today. We were out early."
He raised his brows at Roberts. "What did the ladies
do?"

"Had breakfast in the public dining room, then
went out!"

"Is there anything that could be misconstrued?
Were they here at the same time as my stepmother?"

Roberts shook his head decisively. "Definitely not!
The wife says the elder one went to ask if the terriers
were still shut up as soon as they got back, and that
was some time after!"

"I wonder, can it have something to do with my
dear sister's coming," Mr. Travers pondered. "It is difficult to see how, but it is the only other happening of
note. What mistaken inferences could Vanessa have
drawn from that?"

He thought back carefully over the scene in the
hall. He had bundled Caroline into the coffee room
before, he thought, there had been a chance for them
to be observed, but it was quite possible that Vanessa
had seen them, though in itself this did not seem sufficient reason for a precipitous flight. After a few pithy
words with his sister, during which, from the flutter-
ing of her eyelashes in Lord Pendril's direction he
confirmed his suspicion that the object of the visit
was not solely to inspect Vanessa, he and Lord Pendril
had ridden part of the way back with her.

He could not see anything in this to give rise to
such an extreme reaction, and he said finally, "I confess it has me at a stand! How long will Miss Helen's
illness force them to remain?"

Roberts pursed his lips. "She was mortal bad when
I first saw her—I thought she was a goner this time for
sure! The doctor says she's in no danger though, and

her sister says she's picking up remarkable. Still, I should say it will be a couple of days at the least before they dare think of travel."

"Then we have a breathing space! The one we need now is Patty!"

Roberts grinned at Lord Pendril, whom he now regarded in very much the same light as Mr. Travers. "Myself, I'd say you were in some trouble there!"

"Eh? What have I done?" Lord Pendril said, startled.

"You being out when she came down to luncheon, she took that little dog for a walk down to the village while she was waiting for you and it was set on by the gypsies' dogs on the green!"

A hopeful gleam appeared in Lord Pendril's eye. "Did they see it off?"

Roberts shook his head. "There's naught wrong with it, barring a fright and its fur being a bit wet where they mauled it."

Plainly disappointed, Lord Pendril said, "Well, she can hardly blame that on to me!"

"It seems she does!" Seeing Lord Pendril's expression of puzzlement, he shrugged. "You know what females are! She says if you'd been where you were supposed to be, she'd never have gone out and it wouldn't have happened!"

Lord Pendril nodded gloomily. "That follows!" He looked across to Mr. Travers. "You might need her, dear boy, but I think I'll keep out of her way until she's cooled down!"

Mr. Travers therefore dispatched a chambermaid to ask Patty to meet him in the private parlor if it was convenient and went down to await her. A few moments later the maid came back, somewhat flustered, bearing the unequivocal reply that it wasn't convenient. Not altogether surprised, Mr. Travers sighed and made his way to her room.

Halfway through his tentative knock she flung back the door and said shortly, "No!"

"Patty, be reasonable!" he pleaded. "You're surely not holding me responsible!"

"You're every bit as much to blame as Charles! You both go off, leaving me for the entire day . . ."

Insinuating himself through the door, Mr. Travers said apologetically, "I am afraid that *was* my fault. When we got back from our fishing we discovered there had been some excitement! My stepmother had been here while we were away, and then on top of that, Caroline came!"

Patty had opened her mouth to continue her complaints, but she paused at this, and Mr. Travers went on, "But that is only half the story. I need your help!"

Patty's chief, and some said her only, virtue was that she was undoubtedly kindhearted, and an appeal for help seldom left her unmoved. Picking up the woebegone Jason, she kicked off her slippers, exposing a generous expanse of ankle, and settled herself comfortably on the bed while Mr. Travers began his recital.

When he had finished she leaned back and regarded him with affectionate scorn. "All I can say is it's your own fault! You can bet your last sixpence that it's got something to do with this silly caper you've set up! Still, that's neither here nor there at the moment. I take it you want me to see if I can find out what it's all about."

"I should be most grateful. If you went to inquire how Helen goes on, you could perhaps say you saw their luggage being carried down, which would save involving Roberts."

Patty snorted. "Why should I consider Roberts! He ran to you fast enough with his tale! Still, I'll see what I can do. It goes against the grain to betray my own sex, but if they've taken some silly notion into their heads I'll do what I can to put it right. All supposing they'll tell me what it is, which there's no reason why they should!"

This was Mr. Travers's private doubt and it proved to be well founded. When Patty, full of good intentions, called at their room, she found Helen asleep and Vanessa uncommunicative. It was hardly possible during their whispered dialogue at the door to drop in the point about the luggage, and Patty retired to report defeat. Roberts conveyed the information that Vanessa had had a light meal and some soup and hot milk sent up, and Mr. Travers rightly concluded that they would see nothing more of her that day.

However, by ten o'clock the next morning he judged she would have no excuse to deny him admittance. Walking along the corridor, he was not quite sure what his own sentiments were. Disappointment was there, and, he had to admit, more than a touch of annoyance. His pride, as well as his feelings, was wounded. Miss Vanessa Hartland had intended to deal him the most profound and deliberate snub—she could not even stay to say good-bye to the one whom the Lady Elizabeth Gnosill so eagerly awaited up at the Court. She did not know what she dismissed so lightly! At this point it dawned on Mr. Travers that what Vanessa was dismissing so lightly was precisely what he had been at such pains to suppress, and he could hardly complain if he discovered that her evaluation of his true worth did not match up to his own. He paused, a wry smile twisting his lips. He had always considered himself the reverse of conceited. London abounded with men who held themselves in high esteem with little cause and he had always regarded them with faint contempt, but how, after all, was he to know how others viewed him? Perhaps the various stratagems employed by so many mamas to bring their daughters to his notice had colored his opinion of himself. He had cynically presumed that his possessions, not his person, formed the main attraction for the matchmakers, therefore to find his assumption had been correct ought not to ruffle his equanimity.

He thus arrived at Vanessa's door in a rather more chastened frame of mind than he had set out with, while for her part she greeted him with confusion. She and Helen had agreed over their morning chocolate to treat Mr. Travers with friendly reserve so that there should not be any awkwardness during the remainder of their stay, but such was her dread that he might already have learned of their intended flight that she could hardly raise her eyes to his face. She murmured that it was good of him to come but after that was stricken with dumbness and led the way to where Helen, now dressed, sat by the window.

Mr. Travers, taking Helen's hand, found the last lingering traces of annoyance dissipated. Whatever the reason for their strange conduct it was plain that Helen was still unwell and both were extremely embarrassed in his presence.

Smiling, he said, "I understand Roberts's parrot is to blame for this!"

In spite of herself, Helen could not remain unaffected by his smile and easy greeting. She said, "So it would appear, sir. It seems incredible, but the doctor assured my sister that it was the cause. I am glad to know it because it is something that it is simple to avoid in the future."

"And this particular culprit has been removed and the coffee room well aired so you may venture in there without fear when you come down."

She turned her head and stared out over the apple trees in the orchard. "I do not think it will be today, Mr. Travers."

"Why, no, if you do not feel sufficiently recovered, but we shall expect you tomorrow!"

Helen stirred uncomfortably in her chair, and knowing she was incapable of telling a direct lie, Vanessa said quickly, "Of course she will be down, Mr. Travers, but as soon as she is well enough we must think of getting on our way. After all, it is only by accident that we are here at all. We had planned to be in London at this moment."

"But you have said there is no one expecting you so there cannot be any necessity for haste. I thought you were finding your stay here pleasant!"

In some confusion, she said, "Why, yes, but that is not the point. No matter how pleasant, we cannot afford to be lingering here. I once confided my—my plans to you, and it is time and more that we embarked on them."

She had been avoiding his eyes, but she looked up now to find his level gaze on her. "Miss Vanessa, have I offended you in some way?" he asked directly.

"How could you have, sir?"

"That is what I wish you will tell me!"

She attempted a light laugh. "This is nonsense, Mr. Travers!"

Gently, he said, "Perhaps it is, but if I have displeased you, I hope you will give me the opportunity to make amends. Believe me, I have found great pleasure in your company and I should not like anything to mar it."

Vanessa could only bow her head, and after glancing from one to the other, he quietly withdrew. Though she had refused to answer his question and was still determined to leave the Angel, he derived some satisfaction from their exchange. Vanessa was not filled with joyous anticipation by the thought of departure.

He found, however, that she steadfastly avoided his company. When he sent up a message inviting them to join him for luncheon she returned the answer that it would be better for Helen to take it in their room as she was still a little weak. He allowed two hours to elapse and sent up a similar request for tea—she thanked him but they had already taken it. Mr. Travers began to think he would run out of meals in the day before he managed to lure them out, and in the end it was Patty to whom he was indebted for their emergence. Bustling into the room a short while afterward, she declared it was bad for them to be cooped up in the heat when there was a refreshing breeze outside. She had some chairs and a table carried into the orchard and supervised their disposal under the shade of a large pear tree, then went back upstairs to make sure that Vanessa and Helen took advantage of her efforts.

Truth to tell, Vanessa was by this time heartily tired of the four walls of the bedchamber and needed little urging. The orchard was pleasantly private, surrounded as it was by a high stone wall with ivy growing profusely over it, and she and Helen sat under the tree with their books, occasionally glancing up to watch the butterflies in their erratic flight over the flowers. They passed an hour in peaceful enjoyment and she was just thinking of going into the inn to ask for some lemonade to be sent out to them when an excited barking heralded the approach of Barnaby and Patch. They dashed up to Helen, ignoring any claims Vanessa might have on their attention, and as she laughingly tried to prevent them from jumping on her lap to lick her face, Vanessa, with the premonition that they would not be alone, looked around to behold Lord Pendril and Mr. Travers coming through the gate. Her first thought was that Patty must have told of their whereabouts, but it proved to be the keen tracking instincts of the terriers that was to blame. They ran back to Lord Pendril, proudly asking him to see who they had found, then returned to sit under the shade of Helen's chair, panting gently from their exertions.

"So this is where you were hiding yourselves!" Lord Pendril said, coming over. He ran a finger inside his wilting shirt collar and lowered himself unceremoniously on to the grass between them. "By God, it's hot! You girls must be parched!"

Taking the hint, Mr. Travers grinned and went back to order refreshments, and Lord Pendril was just telling the terriers that it would have been a dashed good thing if they'd got at Roberts's bird before it had a chance to make Miss Helen ill, when ignoring him for once, they dashed off across the orchard to announce that danger threatened from the other side of the wall.

With no presentiment of doom, Lord Pendril went
to peer over and stood rooted to the spot as his de-
spairing gaze fell on the cause of their insistent barking. Gaily waving a hand in greeting, Caroline turned
her horse toward him, her face under the dashing hat
wearing a provocative smile.

"Charles! How does one get in there and I'll come
and join you!"

Chapter Six

"No, no!" Lord Pendril exclaimed hastily. At Caroline's look of surprise, he said, "What I mean is—well, it's a bit awkward at the moment!" Indulging the hope that Caroline might not be visible from the far side of the orchard he glanced quickly behind him, but both Helen and Vanessa were regarding the newcomer with a curious expression.

Following the direction of his eyes, Caroline said gaily, "Oh, you have company!"

"Yes," Lord Pendril said, resignation settling on him. She had a clear, carrying voice and he had no difficulty in imagining the remarks hovering on her tongue. "I'll come around and meet you in the courtyard. Wait for me there!" He tried to invest his last words with a warning, but Caroline only gave him another sunny smile before trotting off down the road, and his brain a paralyzed blank he turned back to Helen and Vanessa.

Though not overperceptive, it struck him that there

was something strained in their attitudes and carefully schooled features. Vanessa sat rigidly immobile and it was Helen who asked, "Who was that, Lord Pendril? I believe I caught a glimpse of her yesterday."

Lord Pendril cleared his throat. "Miss Caroline," he said lamely. Feeling their eyes on him as they waited for further information, he searched his mind desperately for an acceptable explanation, then the answer came to him, astounding him with its brilliance. "Miss Caroline Harmer! She's George's sister from up at the Court!"

Vanessa only stared at him, the color draining from her face, and Helen's gentle voice once more broke the silence. "She is the one who lent her riding habit to Vanessa?"

"That's right! Very obliging girl—I've known her for years! Quentin has too, of course!" Anxious to get away to coach Caroline in her new role, he did not wait for further questions, and thus did not see the glances they exchanged.

For a long time neither of them spoke. Vanessa's fingers twisted in the folds of her gown, betraying her agitated thoughts, and she finally raised imploring eyes to Helen.

"I don't understand," she said helplessly. "I just cannot understand! I was so sure . . ." She cast her mind back over what she had seen and heard in the hall, searching for any other explanation. If she had indeed misunderstood the matter then she had almost robbed Helen of her future happiness. "The landlord said Mr. Travers's mother-in-law had been here, and the way they spoke of it—something Mr. Travers said in particular made me think—and then when that girl ran up to him and kissed him, I naturally presumed . . . Oh Helen, it seems I was wrong all the time!" The enormity of the mistake and what had so nearly resulted from it made her mind whirl and shattered all her confidence in her judgment. From the moment when she had decided they must sell the house she had been so sure she was capable of dealing with any situation. Helen's doubts she had swept aside as the products of a nervous imagination, and because she had been in the habit for some years of making decisions for both of them she had come to believe she must always be right. Now, for the first time, she began to wonder if she was not merely odiously managing.

"Vanessa." Helen's quiet voice broke in on her chaotic reflections and she looked up. "The reference you heard to Mr. Travers's mother-in-law—could it not mean his stepmother? Why she should be here and what Lord Pendril meant by his remark I do not pretend to understand, but it may well have nothing to do with us at all."

"I know! I know! I realize it now! Everything conspired at the time to point to the one interpretation, but if I had only mentioned it to Mr. Travers instead . . ." She shrugged. "But I had occasionally thought before that he was deliberately practicing some sort of concealment! We have told him a great deal about ourselves, yet with all the time we have spent in his company we know no more of him than what I learned on that first morning. It seemed strange to me that he never spoke of his house or his family and it began to look as though he did not *want* us to know anything about him and . . ." She broke off, a rueful smile narrowing her eyes. "There! I am raising suspicions again! If Miss Harmer knows him so well and comes here openly, there cannot be anything discreditable!"

The supposed Miss Harmer was at that moment in the courtyard where she had encountered Mr. Travers and was lending an unrepentant ear to his strictures. His opinion of her forward conduct she heard out in an amiable and appreciative silence, merely remarking, "Very true!" at the end of it.

Mr. Travers drew a long breath. "Would you mind paying a little more attention to the rest of what I have to say, otherwise you will ruin everything! You are Miss Caroline Harmer and you live at the Court. Charles and I frequently come to stay with your brother, George, who has been called away at the moment."

"Why has he been called away?" Caroline inquired, in a practical spirit.

"It doesn't matter. I leave it to your powers of invention. At the moment you have guests, and . . ."

"That's true," Caroline agreed. "Though they are leaving tomorrow. Mama is prostrate with relief!"

"Let us hope the experience will teach her not to repeat her efforts," Mr. Travers said unkindly.

"She can't very well if you are going to . . ." She paused, catching his eye. "I know what you are going to say! They are merely breaking their journey! Quentin, you cannot honestly expect me to continue to believe in all that nonsense! You don't tell all those untruths—yes, and get me to tell them as well—for a girl in whom you have only a passing interest! If she was leaving soon and you were never likely to see her again, it wouldn't matter if she thought you were the richest man in England! Is she very beautiful? Shall I like her?"

"Once I am convinced that you can play your part you will have an opportunity to judge for yourself," Mr. Travers said patiently. "*Will* you pay attention!"

She gave him a demure look. "Of course! Where were you?"

"I am fast losing track of it myself! Can you remember it so far?"

She repeated what he had told her and he nodded. "Good. Now for the rest! I went to the Court a few days ago, but George had been called away and your mother had guests, so I came to Priors Cross and put up here. You saw me the day before yesterday when I came to borrow the riding habit for Vanessa, and you had better admit, if it is mentioned, that you were here yesterday. You may have been seen—in fact I'm almost certain you were. I don't think there's much more. It is best to keep it as simple as possible, and don't let your enthusiasm carry you away! You have never visited my home, and I live—it had better be somewhere not too far away—just outside Warwick Hall will do. Stay with the truth as far as possible. We shall be less likely to contradict one another and you will find it easier to remember!"

Caroline grinned at him. "Dear brother, don't you think I've had a *tiny* bit of practice before now?" She bestowed a melting look on Lord Pendril, who was coming across the courtyard toward them. "But you had better warn Charles that you haven't any brothers or sisters and that you live near Warwick. I doubt if he knows!"

The information was passed on to Lord Pendril, who had been up to warn Patty of the current situation. He swore, begged Caroline's pardon, and returned to instruct Patty in the latest developments.

This, not unnaturally, had the effect of bringing her down as well, and as he viewed the party that presently made its way to the orchard Mr. Travers very nearly resolved on a full confession to avoid the pitfalls he could see looming ahead.

In addition to his apprehension, his fingers itched to chastise Caroline. She, notwithstanding Patty's presence, was making shameless sheep's eyes at his lordship, and because of the masquerade Mr. Travers was powerless to check her.

But though he little knew it, nothing could have surely driven away the last vestiges of Vanessa's doubts than Caroline's behavior. Observing the sidelong glances she cast at Lord Pendril from under her long lashes, Vanessa was quickly convinced that her first impression had been entirely erroneous, and a quick glance confirmed that her left hand was bare of rings. Now that it was so palpably obvious that they were not married, she wondered how she could have been so foolish as to suppose it in the first place.

She and Helen rose as the party approached, and the newcomer was presented to them, Caroline expressing the hope that the habit had proved a reasonable fit.

"Indeed, yes," Vanessa said warmly. "I wrote a note that Mr. Travers promised to deliver to you, but I am glad to have the opportunity of thanking you in person. I did not think to meet with such kindness as I have received from you and your brother!"

Frantically trying to grasp the substance of this last part, Caroline cast a glance of mute appeal at Mr. Travers, but it was Lord Pendril who rose nobly to the occasion.

"Always ready to lend his horses, George," he said.

"Once let me have a hunter for the whole of the season."

Relieved to have the matter made clear, Caroline said brightly, "But that was nothing! And how churlish of George it would be not to do so when he cannot possibly use them all himself! How do you like Hussein? Is he not a delightful ride?"

Mr. Travers's eyes glinted at this oblique attack. Presumably Walker had informed her that he was not pleased to discover she had been using the little Arab in his absence. But Vanessa was agreeing that there could be no more perfect horse, and Mr. Travers, the hair rising lightly on the back of his neck, heard Caroline propose that they should all go out together the following morning.

He could only foresee disaster resulting from such a length of time spent in each other's company, and he said, "Do not allow her to press you if you do not feel up to it, Miss Helen. You were extremely ill only yesterday."

He tried to fix Caroline with a repressive look. To his annoyance it went wide of its mark where his sister was concerned, but, he suspected, was intercepted by Vanessa. He could only hope she would take the statement at its face value, and meanwhile Caroline had turned to Helen and was saying impulsively, "Oh, do not say you will not be well enough! It would be so pleasant!"

Helen hesitated, clearly not liking to refuse her, and Mr. Travers seized the chance to point out that they lacked mounts for Lord Pendril and Patty.

Airily, Caroline said, "But that need not present any difficulty!" She dimpled at his helplessness, before adding, "Walker may bring them down!"

Nursing revengeful thoughts, Mr. Travers held his peace. Walker would pale at the prospect of returning to filch yet two more horses and Roberts might say with truth that he had nowhere left to stable them; but the circumstances hardly seemed worthy of mention since he had no doubt that Caroline was quite ready to overcome such trifling impediments as the fact that her mother's guests were departing next morning and the most ordinary civility demanded that she should be present to see them off. Also, as far as he was aware, Helen was currently in possession of Patty's only riding habit. He was reluctant to raise further objections in case he aroused Vanessa's suspicions but this last seemed a legitimate barrier to the scheme. Unfortunately he knew it was one Caroline was unlikely to regard. Intent on pursuing Lord Pendril in spite of his unencouraging response, she would not regard Patty's inability to join them as an unsuperable obstacle to the expedition.

He was relieved a moment later when Helen raised the question herself, but to his deep disappointment, Patty was equipped with a second one. He reflected that no other female of his acquaintance would pack two habits for a comparatively short stay at an inn where there were no riding horses available. In an undervoice he observed as much to Patty and she informed him candidly that it had been in the expectation of using his own horses that she had brought them since Lord Pendril had presumed that he would be staying at the Court and taking advantage of the usual amenities.

For some unknown reason this mitigated Mr. Travers's desire to strangle his sister and restored his good humor. He knew he had brought the whole thing on himself when he embarked on the pretense, and he should have known better than to place any reliance on the discretion of a volatile damsel of only seventeen summers. Once again he almost made up his mind to tell Vanessa the whole, but with the decision half formed he had a brief picture of the determination in her small face when she had outlined her ambitions that morning down by the river. Without undue conceit he felt he could supply all the benefits she envisaged in the alliance with her merchant, without, moreover, any of the irksome disadvantages. If he courted her in the normal manner, took her to his home and introduced her to his stepmother, she would be influenced by her surroundings no less than any of the other young women invited over the last few years. Too often had he seen the expression in their eyes as they traversed the marble entrance hall, and he felt it was extremely unfair of the fates to have deposited Vanessa in the vicinity of so much temptation. On the other hand, if the fortuitous attack of asthma had occurred twenty miles farther along their route . . .

Here Mr. Travers stopped to examine his thoughts. Only two days ago he had told Lord Pendril he could not be sure of his precise intentions, but as he looked across at Vanessa they were suddenly clear. It was not her undeniable beauty that attracted him—he could appreciate it, and imagine the pride he would take in her, but he had never placed perfection of features at the top of his requirements, and he admitted that of the two sisters, Helen had a gentler, more charming disposition. Vanessa, in fact, he sometimes found a little too decided in her opinions, which was not a trait he had ever found appealing in the past. Considering her dispassionately he concluded that he had met girls before as attractive, even though not as beautiful, and definitely most of them would rank above her by conventional standards of social behavior and decorum. But none of those handsome, well-trained young ladies had stirred his emotions in the slightest, and Mr. Travers could only assume that what he was experiencing must be love. He could think of no other reason for his desire to cherish and protect from the world a girl whom reason told him was quite capable of fending for herself and could quite easily achieve the goal she had set herself.

Whether she would have the same success in her aims for her sister he was not so certain—he had a suspicion that their aspirations were not the same. Several times he had noted a subtle change in Helen when Lord Pendril was present. Her face would become more alive, and her eyes turned more frequently toward him than to the other members of the company. But nothing was more certain than that Lord Pendril was totally unaware of her regard. For a moment Mr. Travers toyed with the idea of dropping him a hint, then rejected it. Helen would not like it known, and it might even cause Lord Pendril embarrassment. His appearance at a London ball, where he was known for a dangerous rake, could, and did, strike terror into the hearts of mothers bent on getting their daughters suitably established, but Lord Pendril knew Helen was in a very different category from those sophisticated and worldly young women. He had his own private codes and he would no more dream of embarking on an affair with her than he would of riding his hunters in the summer.

Sadly, Mr. Travers could not foresee a happy outcome. From regarding her with sympathy, his gaze became abstracted; but to Vanessa, glancing up, it seemed only that he could not tear his eyes away from Helen's face. Jubilation swept over her, but behind it a small pain tugged, sharp, and by now familiar. As on previous occasions she refused to let her mind recognize it or even acknowledge its presence, and she managed to continue her conversation with unabated cheerfulness.

So successfully did she hide that ache that Caroline, thinking that matters were in a fair way to being settled with her brother, forgot her role to the extent of saying she thought they were going to be great friends. She was recalled by a quick frown from Mr. Travers and added hurriedly, "How foolish of me when of course you are not staying! But we shall be great friends during the next few days, I know!" She got to her feet, brushing the bits of grass from her skirt. "I must go, or Mama will be wondering what has become of me. Good-bye until tomorrow, and you must each of you pray that the weather holds fine for us! Quentin, come with me and advise me on which of my brother's horses I should send down!"

Obediently, Mr. Travers accompanied her, though once beyond the gate he abandoned his formal courtesy and told her roundly that she was shameless and unprincipled and totally wanting in delicacy.

"I know," she agreed, unabashed. "Mama is forever telling me the same thing!"

"And what is more," Mr. Travers continued, having only half finished his lecture, "you need not think that there is the remotest possibility of attaching Charles with your wiles so you will oblige me by ceasing your attempts! Quite apart from having known you from the cradle, he has no interest in schoolgirls!"

"I am *not* a schoolgirl!" Caroline retorted, roused. "*Several* people have been excessively surprised to learn that I have not yet been presented, which I shall be next year anyway! Besides, in only two years time, I shall be nineteen!"

Impatiently, Mr. Travers said, "All this is beside the point!"

"No it isn't!" she returned. "Vanessa is only nineteen! I asked her!"

His face relaxed. "Touché! Nevertheless, my child, as you will learn, there is a vast difference between seventeen and nineteen. You are not very old, and you know perfectly well that your mama would not approve of your coming down here. Let tomorrow be the last time!"

Caroline wrinkled her nose at him. "You are only saying that because you are afraid I may say the wrong thing in front of Vanessa! *I* know!" Almost shyly, she added, "But I shan't, I promise you. I wouldn't do anything to spoil your chances."

"Not intentionally, but you will admit that you're scatterbrained!"

"Yes, but not *nearly* as much as I used to be!" In a wistful voice she said irrelevantly, "I wish I had black hair and great long eyelashes."

Though inwardly amused, Mr. Travers felt it was time to be brutal. "It would avail you nothing! Charles has no interest in Vanessa either!"

"No, he hasn't," Caroline agreed, much cheered. "It is excessively odd because I have never seen anyone so lovely."

Mr. Travers ruffled her curls. "One of the things

you discover as you grow older is that a man of sense seeks other things besides a lovely face. Now put your hat back on! You look an absolute hoyden!"

Settling it on her head, Caroline said doubtfully, "I'm not at all certain that I want a man of sense. It sounds rather dull!"

"Fortunate, my child, because I shouldn't think one could be induced to take you!" He consulted the watch at his waist. "And it is time you were back home. What tale are you going to tell your mama to account for your absence?"

She chuckled. "Oh, I shall think of something, never fear!"

As he wended his way back to the orchard, Mr. Travers had no doubt that she would. He pondered on whether to hint to his stepmother that it might be advisable to keep a closer watch on her excursions, then he had a mental picture of her reaction if she were to find out that he was allowing her daughter to form one of a party that included an actress widely known for her activities off the stage. Patty's philosophy for life, he felt, was not one that would recommend itself to Mrs. Travers as suitable for an impressionable girl.

He was still grinning to himself when he reached the orchard gate, and as it creaked open, Vanessa and Helen looked up and smiled back. It struck him that they were noticeably more relaxed than when he had left them, while Lord Pendril, on the other hand, wore the expression of a man who would rather be elsewhere.

There was no opportunity to inquire the cause of the viscount, and it was Patty who enlightened him. Drawing him to one side, she told him, "You're never here when you're needed!"

His eyes resting on Lord Pendril, he said, "I had sensed that there was something amiss! I take it, however, that whatever it was has been satisfactorily overcome!"

Patty nodded. "And as it turns out, some good has come of it. I think I've found out why they tried to make off yesterday!" At Mr. Travers's sharpened interest, she said significantly, "They thought you were married!"

"What!" Mr. Travers exclaimed, startled out of his caution.

"Sh-h! They'll know what we're talking about! I can't be certain, because naturally nothing was actually said, but it appears Vanessa overheard Roberts telling you your mother-in-law had been here, and it doesn't seem to have crossed her mind he meant your stepmother. Myself, I'd say she was a bit hasty to straightaway think you must be married," she added critically. "Unless, of course, there was more to it than that!"

"There was—oh, there was!" Mr. Travers groaned. "I can see what she must have thought!" Meeting Patty's expression of open curiosity, he said, "To anyone listening, the whole conversation would reek of a diabolical conspiracy! Roberts warned me that my *mother-in-law* didn't believe him when he told her I'd left, and that she would probably be back! His very manner of telling me would seem suspicious, and then to crown it all, I remember I cursed and said I'd only needed a few more days!"

"A few more days . . ." For a moment Patty looked blank, then she stared at him in amazement. "Are you telling me that she thought you intended to try to seduce her?"

"Thank you, Patty! Your astonishment restores my self-esteem! No, but consider! They have never left their home village before, and they were largely brought up by a nanny, who, if my acquaintance with nannies is anything to judge by, would have spent most of her time warning them to beware the wicked wiles of men!"

"Yes, but . . ." Patty broke off, then nodded slowly. "I suppose it could seem that way. And it's no secret the terms I'm on with Charles, which wouldn't help them to think otherwise!"

Trying to pinpoint in his mind the details of the conversation with Roberts, Mr. Travers said, "And there's more! Charles turned craven and said there was no point in staying on here if we had been discovered! Oh, I can understand it all now—it would sound absolutely damning!"

"Trust Charles to drive the last nail home! It's a good thing we were able to clear it up! If it hadn't been for Vanessa asking him how your mother-in-law came to be here we should never have known!"

Appreciatively, Mr. Travers observed, "I'll wager that put him all on end!"

"It did, but he kept his head! As a matter of fact, he told her the truth, which," Patty admitted, "is more than I would have thought to do on the spur of the moment."

"He did *what*?"

She patted his arm soothingly. "No, no! Not all of it—just the part about your stepmother trying to arrange a marriage for you with a woman you didn't fancy. He said she was making your life a misery so you'd gone into hiding until the whole thing should have blown over. If they think about it hard it doesn't explain everything completely, but it's up to you to work the rest out for yourself. After all, you started the whole business."

"Yes," Mr. Travers said ruefully. "I did."

She viewed him thoughtfully. "You're going to get into more trouble if you keep it up. For goodness' sake, tell the girl the truth!"

"Just a little longer, Patty, until I'm sure."

"Well, if you want my opinion, you're taking a risk!"

"I know, but we have survived all the alarms so far."

"I didn't mean that! It's the girl I'm thinking about, not you! She's hardly going to be flattered when she does find out, which is something you don't seem to have considered!"

"Ah, but for that I have an unassailable defense," Mr. Travers said, smiling gently.

She gave a skeptical sniff. "It's to be hoped you have—you'll need one! You've still a lot to learn about women!"

This Mr. Travers was willing to admit and he would have given much to be able to see into Vanessa's mind. Relieved though he was at Patty's information, it still did not tell him whether she had tried to leave because she had taken fright at the apparent implications of what she had overheard, or whether she had formed a regard for him and felt it best to remove herself from his vicinity if he was married. He could only hope it was the latter, but though he had Helen's word that she was not indifferent to him, neither by word nor gesture had she ever given him any encouragement.

He looked across to where she sat under the pear tree, the shadows of the leaves making a moving pat-

tern on the white of her gown. In spite of all her efforts to protect herself from the sun, the last few days
had given her skin a warm glow, which added to her
attractiveness. Watching her, he wondered idly why
fashionable women should have such a passion for
painting themselves with white at the first touch of
the sun, and in the middle of his ponderings she
glanced up and smiled at him in unaffected friendli-
ness.

He walked over to lower himself by her chair, and
she said, "Miss Harmer is the kindest girl! She is
bringing me a hat for tomorrow as well. I feel guilty
about accepting so much from a stranger."

"There is no need to," Mr. Travers said lightly. "I
have helped her out of a good many scrapes when she
was younger. And probably will do again," he added.
"She's a madcap!"

Vanessa breathed more easily at his tone. Hard
upon the relief of finding that Mr. Travers was not,
after all, married to Caroline had come the realization
that it was not unlikely that he should be considering
it. She was the sister of his friend, extremely pretty
and obviously in good circumstances, and there would
have been ample opportunity for him to develop a
fondness for her.

Unconsciously comforting her still further, Mr.
Travers said, "I've known her all her life, you know.
We have been almost like brother and sister."

It occurred to Vanessa that Caroline did not seem
to regard Lord Pendril in quite the same fraternal
spirit, but she dismissed the thought as unimportant.
It was not Lord Pendril but Mr. Travers she was concerned with—Mr. Travers whom she had so grossly
misjudged! Shame overwhelmed her again. Viewing

her actions in retrospect, she could not imagine how she could have allowed herself to harbor such terrible ideas about a gentleman who had never shown them anything but kindness. And if Mr. Travers should ever find out . . . It came to her suddenly that Mr. Travers could hardly fail to. Even if Roberts refrained from telling him, there were a host of other people who had probably been aware of their intention. Their trunk had stood in the hall for anyone to see; the postboy would naturally have grumbled to his colleagues when the chaise was not, after all, required; a chambermaid would have been instructed to clear their room. The very fact that their departure had been prevented by Helen's illness would make it a talking point.

"Miss Vanessa," Mr. Travers said patiently, "I have twice desired to know if you would like me to procure you a glass of lemonade. Let me tell you that I am not accustomed to such churlish disregard!"

She raised startled eyes to his face. "No—no thank you! I beg your pardon if I was not attending, but . . ." Resolutely, she straightened her shoulders. "Mr. Travers, I should like to talk to you privately!"

"Now?" he inquired, surprised.

Firmly, she said, "Now!" knowing that if she postponed the deed and allowed herself time to think about it, she would never gather together sufficient courage to broach it again.

"Very well," Mr. Travers said. "Do you wish me to announce that we are taking a stroll down to the spinney, or will it be enough if we merely go and examine the magpie's nest at the far end of the orchard?"

Vanessa thought that if they went to the spinney Lord Pendril would very likely decide to bring the terriers. In a small voice, she said, "The magpie's nest will do."

Mr. Travers offered his arm, but though she succeeded in stiffening her knees, her inner turmoil was betrayed by the tremor in her fingers. Already regretting her resolve, she wondered desperately how on earth she could make her confession and at the same time avoid telling him she hoped he would shortly be making her sister an offer. There was no way that she could see. It was yet another example, she thought bitterly, of how her own impulsiveness led her into trouble.

At her side, Mr. Travers wrestled with the problem from another angle. A moment's reflection told him there could be only one matter of importance about which Vanessa could wish to speak to him in private, and he was as little anxious to hear the confession as Vanessa was to make it. Patty's recent words came back to him with force and for the first time he appreciated her argument. What had seemed, in the light of his previous experiences, to be merely a reasonable precaution, now struck him as a cheap and slighting charade. Vanessa would be justifiably affronted when she discovered it, the more so if he allowed her to go on with what she was preparing herself to say.

Both occupied with their differing aspects of the dilemma they had reached the end of the orchard where the magpie chattered angrily at them from the lower bough of his domain. Incensed at the intrusion of his territory he hopped clumsily back and forth, but Vanessa bestowed only a cursory glance in his direction before determinedly rounding to face her companion.

"Mr. Travers . . ." she began.

"Miss Vanessa," he returned. "Before you tell me, may I ask a question? Is this concerned with yesterday?"

Vanessa felt the ground to have opened beneath her feet and she was obliged to swallow several times before she could find her voice. "You—you know?" She faltered, finally.

"Well, yes, but it was a very natural mistake to have made and in a great part it is my own fault! I must apologize for having encouraged you in the error. I hope you will forgive me."

Vanessa stared at him, too thankful to try to work out why she, who had nerved herself to sue for pardon, should now be receiving an apology from Mr. Travers. Bemused, she stammered, "I'm—I'm sure there can be nothing to forgive."

"There is a great deal!" He paused, knowing he should make his own confession now, but he was suddenly afraid she would turn from him in disgust. On the other hand, there was tomorrow's riding expedition to be got through with the ever-present risk that Caroline's unwary tongue might give him away, and in circumstances under which it would be far more difficult to give his explanation.

But if he were to ask her to marry him now? He found that as plain Mr. Travers, bereft of his possessions, he was considerably less confident of her reply, but this, after all, was what he had intended to discover.

She was still gazing up at him, her head tilted to one side in inquiry. Vaguely he was aware that the magpie had flown to the ground and was screaming abuse from only a few yards away.

He said, "Vanessa . . ." but got no further. Two

black-and-white terriers hurtled by; the magpie
screeched in fear; Vanessa gave a cry of alarm as his
demise seemed certain; and with laboriously flapping
wings the magpie managed to lift himself clear of
their snapping jaws and once more crouched on the
bottom branch whence he mouthed futile threats at
his persecutors.

Unimpressed, both by the violence of its language
and Vanessa's scolding, the terriers hopefully circled
the base of the tree until Lord Pendril appeared. He
called them sternly to order, only marring the effect
of his severity when he added in a congratulatory
tone, "But, by God, you nearly got it!"

Vanessa gave him a reproachful look and he said,
"Magpies, you know. Take the eggs!" Then with rare
tact he withdrew together with Barnaby and Patch to
the other end of the orchard.

Vanessa laughed as she watched them go. "I think
we should move as well. The poor creature in the tree
probably has eggs of its own and we have caused it
quite enough trouble already."

Mr. Travers thought uncharitably that it had caused
him a great deal more—the moment was utterly lost
and only an extremely insensitive man would contemplate putting the question now.

As they turned and began to walk slowly back, Vanessa recalled that he had started to ask her something and remarked innocently, "We were interrupted
by the terriers. What were you about to say, Mr. Travers?"

His lips twitched wryly. "Nothing of importance,"
he said. "It will do another time."

Chapter Seven

Mr. Travers, alert for another opportunity to present his case, was still no further by ten o'clock the following morning when they were due to assemble in the courtyard. By this time, however, he had passed into a fatalistic frame of mind and was more inclined to worry over the effect on his sister of the sight of Lord Pendril in the saddle. If the viscount could wreak havoc in female breasts in the ballroom where he was a notably indifferent performer, then on horseback, where he excelled, the damage would be incalculable.

And it was of no use to remind himself that Caroline had been unmoved by the spectacle the previous Christmas on his last visit. Certainly six months ago his presence had not quickened her pulse one iota, but the transition from sixteen to seventeen had wrought more changes in her than the shearing of her juvenile curls, and Mr. Travers would willingly have done without the responsibility of chaperoning her under circumstances where she well knew that he was shackled.

But ten o'clock came and went without any sign of her, and by twenty past, Mr. Travers was beginning to entertain hopes that she had been prevented from coming. Even Patty, notoriously unpunctual, was present by this time. Her appearance on the scene caused Helen and Vanessa to blink and a disrespectful stableboy to let out a long whistle of amazement, while Mr. Travers offered up heartfelt thanks that she had, after all, seen fit to bestow on Helen the emerald green habit that had caused him such qualms at the time. To be seen abroad in the alternative, a garment of scarlet wool, braided down the front and around the cuffs with gold lace, would, he felt, effectively rob a sensitive girl like Helen of any enjoyment in the expedition.

Even Lord Pendril was moved to expostulate on the proximity of scarlet to Patty's richly auburn locks, declaring that such a devilish combination was enough to frighten the horses. Patty, naturally much offended, retorted that she had bought it to please not him but herself, and that when she felt in need of his opinion she would ask for it.

Mr. Travers found the resultant quarrel a trifle embarrassing as Lord Pendril had no hesitation in pointing out that since he had provided the money for its purchase, it damned well gave him the right to give his opinion. Patty immediately retaliated by informing him, together with the stableboy, two postilions, and the occupants of a coach that had just pulled into the yard, that far from providing the money, the modiste had been dunning her for payment for the last three months; and while she was on the subject, there was the little matter of the pink carriage dress that he had promised to defray the cost of, and for which the same modiste was still impatiently awaiting settlement.

In the pause that followed upon this attack, Mr. Travers heard the stableboy call through the inn door for those inside to come into the yard because the swells were having a turn-up and it was as good as a play. The unheeding protagonists were unlikely to be disturbed by the addition of a couple of chambermaids and waiters to the audience already assembled, but Mr. Travers could feel himself beginning to grow warm inside his collar. Lord Pendril had been unwise enough to bring Jason into the dispute, and he felt it would shortly descend to a level that was not only unfit for the ears of two delicately nurtured girls, but would make them all the talking point at the Angel for several days to come.

It was thus with unexpected relief that he greeted Caroline when she clattered into the courtyard, breathless and flushed, and full of apologies for her lateness.

"Mama made me stay to see Elizabeth and Lady Wrenshaw off," she explained, falling in beside Mr. Travers as the cavalcade presently made its way down the road. "I thought they would *never* go! Their carriage had been standing in the drive a full half hour before Elizabeth could be persuaded to get into it. Apparently she is always ill on long journeys, but one cannot go on expressing sympathy forever! I was nearly ready to ride off and leave them!"

"What prevented you?" Mr. Travers inquired, amused.

"Well, for one thing, Mama would have eaten me

when I got back, and for another, it suddenly occurred to me that they must come along this road and only fancy if we should be coming out of the inn just as they went by!"

It was a point that Mr. Travers had also failed to take into account, and as he showed faint signs of alarm, Caroline added, "It's all right. I gave them ten minutes to be on their way before I started out!"

Mr. Travers could not feel that this was a sufficient margin for error. He was able to imagine numerous exigencies that would necessitate a delay of the same length on the travelers' part, and he could not be comfortable with the thought that the next bend in the road might be hiding two irate and disappointed women who would lose no time in informing his stepmother of his whereabouts. He hoped that her desire to find him would have departed with her guests, but if she discovered he was lodged at the Angel, in her present frame of mind she would undoubtedly give herself the trouble of coming down to vent her frustration on him. Ethical considerations apart, Mr. Travers decided there was a great deal to be said in favor of honesty and a clear conscience. Life was so much more simple.

Leaving Caroline to practice her arts on Lord Pendril, he trotted on to take the lead and direct the party down the first convenient turn off from the post road. It was a move he was later to regret though it had an immediate advantage. With little likelihood of encountering anything more speedy than a hay cart they were able to ride three abreast, which meant he could have Vanessa and Helen on each side and discreetly continue their instruction while his sister was happily engaged in pursuing her one-sided flirtation with

Lord Pendril. Listening with half an ear, Mr. Travers ascertained that her behavior could not yet be termed outrageous and thence gave his full attention to his companions on either hand—his two charming pupils, as Vanessa phrased it with a singular lack of modesty.

With the necessity for confession removed it was plain she was enjoying herself hugely, and he looked down at her now and said, "Well, Miss Vanessa? Is it true that one never loses one's acquired skills?"

Her eyes narrowed in laughter. "Surely, sir, as our preceptor it is for you to say. It would be unbecoming in me to give an opinion on my own progress!"

"What a shy, unassuming young woman you are," he said. "Does she strike you as in need of a set-down, Miss Helen? What shall I tell her?"

"Why, sir, that anyone could give a good account of themselves on such beautifully mannered horses!" Ruefully, she said, "Which I fear is no more than I am doing."

"Nonsense!" he said bracingly. "All you lack is some of your sister's excessive confidence in her own ability!" He glanced at Vanessa. "Which is something I could swiftly deflate with a sharp gallop through the field beside us." She put up her chin at him and he grinned. "The idea does not alarm you? Then perhaps you would like to demonstrate your prowess over the hedge at the far end. Hussein is an excellent jumper!"

"Wretch!" she returned, pulling a face at him. "You will please bear in mind that our previous experience was granted us at a very early age and did not include hedges!" She smiled coaxingly. "But now I have admitted my shortcomings, do you think we are proficient enough to be indulged with a short canter?" She leaned forward to pat Hussein's gleaming neck. "This little lad has been most tolerant, and I promise I would abandon myself to a fall before I would snatch at his mouth."

Mr. Travers raised his brows inquiringly at Helen. "How do you feel, Miss Helen? I should be close beside you."

A little nervously she said she would like to try, and Mr. Travers dropped behind to warn the others to hold their mounts back until he had safely escorted Vanessa and Helen to the top of the field. Lord Pendril obligingly opened the gate for them, and Mr. Travers, on guard in case the stretch of smooth grass should prove too much for Hussein's and Pandora's aristocratic lineage, rode between them, ready to take hold of a bridle at the first sign of excitability. But they proceeded only at a decorous canter and halted obediently for the others to come up to join them. Lord Pendril set the pace, leading them up the far side of the field at a gallop, and as he watched, Mr. Travers realized that it was not only his sister upon whom the viscount's horsemanship was making an impression. Astride the raking, brown gelding, he was the epitome of careless grace, and Mr. Travers saw Helen's eyes follow him wistfully as he wheeled the big horse around, controlling its plunging with one apparently negligent hand.

On Caroline, the force of this picturesque display was more apparent. She had a natural aptitude for riding and had been paid too many compliments not to know that she also appeared to advantage in the saddle. After making sure that Lord Pendril was watching her, she sent her mare into a brisk canter, put her at the neatly layered hedge, and flew over it in fine style.

Lord Pendril called, "Well done!" and, pink with pleasure at having received a commendation from him at last, she bowed her head and gathered up her reins to return by the same means. Unfortunately she reckoned without Patty, who, while extremely tolerant of her efforts to detach his lordship, was not averse to displaying her own mastery. Thundering up the field, she cleared the hedge in an equally polished fashion, thus rather detracting from Caroline's performance.

Mr. Travers, having searched in vain for a way to put Caroline in her place, now perceived the means to do it. Patty's mount was one of the finest jumpers in his stable, and he indicated now that she should bring it back over the gate, an ominously solid structure standing considerably higher than the surrounding hedge.

"Can he do it?" Patty queried, surveying it.

He nodded assent, and she turned and demonstrated to a nicety how to ride a horse at an upright obstacle, taking it slowly and judging her distance perfectly.

"Excellent!" Mr. Travers applauded when she reached them. "Where did you learn to ride, Patty?"

"There are a lot of things I haven't told you, my boy," she returned, flicking him with her whip. "If you must know, I was born on a farm, though I don't care to be reminded of it!"

As he grinned at this unexpected revelation of her past history, she added, "My father was a gentleman farmer, mind you, but he was a strict Methodist and very old-fashioned in his ideas. He used to have us all up at half past five in the mornings!" At Lord Pendril's exclamation of disbelief, she nodded. "It's true! We had to milk the cows. I decided early on that I wasn't suited to the life, so I ran away and went to London!"

Her face took on a reminiscent expression, and Mr. Travers, closely acquainted with her more recent career, coughed to remind her of Helen's and Vanessa's presence.

Her eyes twinkling, she said, "That's when I became an actress, of course," but to Mr. Travers's relief forebore to mention the more questionable aspects of her later life.

While they were talking they had begun to walk their horses slowly back toward the lane, and beyond the hedge to the next field, Caroline, momentarily forgotten, gazed after them forlornly. None of Mr. Travers's representations had impaired her belief that it was only a matter of time before Lord Pendril fell victim to her youthful charms, but she realized now that there was indeed a world of difference between seventeen and nineteen. Dismally, she thought that in all probability he did still regard her as a schoolgirl.

Her lip trembled, and for a moment she toyed with the idea of nursing a secret love, hiding it from the world at large and Lord Pendril in particular, then bursting on him as a sophisticated debutante when he would suddenly behold her with new eyes.

But her practical side immediately pointed out that his lordship spent a large part of his time surrounded by sophisticated debutantes, and to date he had shown a marked preference for the more opulent type of actress. It was also plain that he had discarded any thoughts of marriage in favor of less enduring relationships. Briefly she considered loving him from afar, but this again she rejected almost at once as spiritless and stupid. Fictional heroines who indulged in hopeless passions and spent their lives yearning after some dark and tragic figure had always aroused in her a hearty contempt, quite apart from the fact that it was beyond even her imaginative powers to shape Lord Pendril into the heroic role. The only dark secret he was likely to be hiding was the total of his debts, and she had no doubt he would be perfectly willing to divulge even that if he was able to calculate it.

Regretfully, she decided he was not, after all, a suitable subject for her affections. Handsome he might be, and he definitely had the necessary careless air, but at thirty he was perhaps a little old.

Having made up her mind, she characteristically concentrated on the immediate problem, which was to rejoin the others in the next field with the minium loss of dignity. Recalling her presence at last, they had checked their horses for her to catch up with them. With five pairs of eyes upon her, Caroline viewed the gate that Patty had cleared with such style and ease, and acknowledged that she had been beaten at her own game. It was too high for her own little mare, and to ask her to jump it would be inviting an ignominious refusal. Humiliated, she urged her over the hedge, which by contrast had shrunk to negligible proportions, and trotted up to join them. Lord Pendril once more held the gate open and bowed her through with a flourish, but this gesture depressed her even more, realizing as she now did that it was the gallantry of a man toward his friend's young sister.

Suffering all the pangs of an injured ego she followed Helen and Vanessa into the lane, so lost in her thoughts that she was not at once aware of the lone rider approaching them from the opposite direction. But Mr. Travers, recognizing, though with difficulty,

his neighbor Sir Walter Challiner's eldest son, was
swiftly casting around in his mind for a way to avert
exposure. If they paused for any conversation it was
inevitable that Caroline would be revealed as his sister, but for the life of him he could think of nothing
better than to merely treat the young man to a
friendly "Good morning," and go by without slackening their pace. With this in view he urged his horse on
a little faster, and it seemed at first that he would suc-
ceed. The young man returned his nod and bowed to
the ladies, and they were on the point of passing each
other when his eyes returned to Caroline. An expression of wonder crossed his face, and mesmerized, he
reined his horse back.

Caroline stared back at him in like astonishment.
When she had seen him last he had been about to go
up to Cambridge, and at that time had been a rather
thin youth with a face disfigured by the skin erup-
tions of adolescence. Bemused, she wondered how he
could have been transformed into the broad-
shouldered, handsome figure before her, while for his
part he gazed at her and marveled that such a butter-
fly should have emerged from the chrysalis of his re-
membrance.

Finally, she said, "William!" and Mr. Travers, cursing inwardly, waited for the words that would reveal
his subterfuge.

"Miss . . . Miss Caroline!" the young man
breathed.

Mr. Travers offered up a prayer of gratitude, but
the respite, he knew, was strictly temporary. At any
moment William would come out of his trance and recall the respect due to his seniors or start making civil
inquiries of Caroline about her mother's health. Either

way he was undone and it was obvious there was no getting rid of him until he and Caroline had made plans for some future meeting—after that pregnant moment when their eyes locked, William had turned his horse in their direction, all thoughts of his previous destination forgotten.

Nor, Mr. Travers realized, could he expect any help from Caroline, who was either heedless or totally oblivious of the perils of the situation.

The pause in activities, meanwhile, was getting longer and more noticeable. It appeared that William had officially joined the party, and Mr. Travers reluctantly performed the necessary introductions, his mind shuddering away from the complications this invited. It now seemed of paramount importance that he should discover Vanessa's sentiments toward him and inform her of the true state of affairs before it was revealed to her accidentally. And revealed it soon would be unless he could get rid of William, and preferably his sister as well. Lord Pendril and Patty, with praiseworthy presence of mind, had insinuated themselves between Vanessa and Helen and the smitten pair, and Mr. Travers managed to get the group moving again, but already his straining ears had caught one reference to Mrs. Travers.

From the snatches of their conversation he deduced that William was making arrangements to call on his stepmother, but Mr. Travers was troubled by the fear that he might decide that as Caroline's official guardian, he himself was the most proper person to make the representations to. It was becoming increasingly urgent that he should contrive their departure. Vanessa and Helen, though politely hiding their interest, were watching them with the sentimental smiles com-

mon to women witnessing the blossoming of youthful
love, and it would not be long before it was borne on
them that there was a certain oddity in the situation.
Cursing the mischance that had brought him down
this particular lane, Mr. Travers twisted in his saddle
and said pointedly, "You must have a great deal to
talk about, but I am afraid we are taking William out
of his way!" As William opened his mouth to utter a
denial, he added hastily, "Why don't you go back with
him, Caroline?"

"Yes—yes, of course," Caroline said, rousing herself
and withdrawing her rapt gaze from William's features. "I can't think how it comes about, living so near
one another, but we haven't met for two years or
more." Belatedly she remembered that she had actually arranged the expedition, and Helen and Vanessa were bound to consider it very strange manners
if she suddenly abandoned it. "Unless William . . ."

Mr. Travers said kindly, "The rest of us will pardon
you, I know. You need not feel obliged to stay on our
account."

Caroline glanced around hesitantly. "If you would
not think it rude of me . . ."

Lord Pendril and Patty made suitable sounds of dis-
claimer while Mr. Travers fumed over her obtuseness.
He tried to catch her eye and failed, and in desperation begged of William to make up her mind for her
and take her away.

William grinned, but he too seemed to feel that extensive apologies were called for and Mr. Travers began to lose hope of ever escaping from the tide of
courtesies.

". . . and give my regards to Mrs. Travers," he

ended punctiliously. "Doubtless I shall be seeing her shortly."

"Yes, yes!" Mr. Travers said, on tenterhooks and hoping he would not be called upon to explain this last part. "Don't let us detain you any longer!" He waved a hand to urge their departure, a gesture that William apparently interpreted as a *carte blanche* to pay his addresses, so that he paused once more to convey his deep sense of obligation and to assure Mr. Travers that Caroline would be safe in his company and would be escorted back to the Court.

Mr. Travers was tempted to tell him that his solicitude was misplaced since she was in the habit of careering all over the countryside without even a groom in attendance. He quelled it, and in an attempt to dispel the air of authority with which William seemed bent on imbuing him, replied that he was sure her mother would be properly grateful.

This proved to be a mistake. William turned a faintly mystified gaze on him, but Caroline, waking to the danger at last, exclaimed, "Good gracious! Between you you make me feel as thought I were back in the nursery!"

Intent on correcting such a gross error, William was inveigled away without realizing it, and Mr. Travers looked down to find Vanessa regarding him, a little puzzled—as well she might be, he thought—as to why he was rather improperly pushing Caroline off on to her new admirer.

In explanation he said smoothly, "A most suitable connection—I know her mother would wish me to encourage it! His father's estate adjoins the Harmer property and the two families have always been on terms of friendship."

She glanced behind to see if she could be overheard, and said doubtfully, "Oh. Isn't Lord Pendril a suitable connection?"

Mr. Travers grinned. "Most eligible! Besides the title he will inherit, his father is a wealthy man, but with Charles one must also consider the major drawback of his aversion to the wedded state!"

As soon as the words were out, he knew that Helen might think they were meant as a warning. Her face was half averted as she studied the countryside behind the hedge, but a telltale flush crept up her cheek confirming the suspicion. Vainly he tried to think of something to illustrate that it was not what he had intended, then he gave a mental shrug. It was of no use to raise hopes that were unlikely to be fulfilled, and it might be that he had unwittingly done her a kindness. With the greatest possible regard for Lord Pendril, Mr. Travers could not, in any case, think he would make a suitable partner for a girl with Helen's excess of sensibility. He wondered again if Vanessa was aware of the direction of her sister's affections and had questioned him about Lord Pendril on her behalf, but she seemed now to have dismissed the matter from her mind. After turning to watch Caroline's neat, blue-clad figure disappear back the way they had come, she said, wistfully, "Miss Harmer is a very dashing young woman, isn't she?"

"Very!" he replied with feeling. "In fact, a shade too dashing for her mother's peace of mind! I should judge it to be the exuberance of youth, however, and she cannot come to very much harm here in the country."

"And she is so pretty and unaffected that people would forgive her most things! I shouldn't think she

will lack for suitors, especially as . . ." She broke off
and looked questioningly across at Mr. Travers. "Is
she something of an heiress? She has never said anything of the sort, but though she speaks so casually of
her home, one gains the impression that it must be
quite palatial! And then her clothes, and her brother's
horses—everything is of the finest!"

Listening to her artless disclosures, Mr. Travers
found the resolve to confess evaporating within him.
Rather shortly, he said, "I believe a considerable sum
was settled on her."

His tone was more abrupt than he intended and she
looked a little surprised. "Oh, dear! I can tell I should
not have asked! Aren't such things spoken of in polite
circles?"

His lips twisted. "Polite society discusses little else!
No, the question was perfectly in order. Did I sound
as though it wasn't?"

She nodded, and greatly daring, said, "I am surprised *you* are not one of her suitors!"

Helen turned a shocked face toward her, and Mr.
Travers, momentarily forgetting that she was supposed to be unrelated to him, showed blank astonishment. "Caroline!" he exclaimed.

"Why not, if she has expectations!"

Mr. Travers wondered if she could indeed be so totally unaware of his feelings. "I can assure you that I
have no interest in heiresses as such," he said.

"Well, one never knows," Vanessa returned. "One
would have to be very strong-minded not to take such
things into account!"

As he silently echoed her sentiments, it occurred to
Mr. Travers that while he had set out to conceal the
extent of his wealth from her, it was not his intention

that she should suspect that he would be unable to provide her with the ordinary comforts of life. By way of information, he said, "I have sufficient means to enable me to live in a manner that has satisfied me until now, and I have never felt any inclination to supplement my income by marrying a fortune."

"Why, here's a lofty tone," Vanessa said cheerfully. "Though I am sure it does you great credit."

"I think it does," Helen said, with gentle dignity. "In my opinion it would be wrong to marry for any other reason that mutual affection and . . . and esteem. I am not saying that one can be happy in poverty—that would be foolish, but it is not necessary that one should be able to command every sort of extravagance."

"Oh, isn't it!" Lord Pendril said, catching them up in time to hear this last. "You tell that to Patty! I shall end up in the Fleet before she's done!" He brought his horse up beside Helen's. "Who's extravagance were you talking about?"

"We weren't," Mr. Travers told him. "Miss Vanessa had been expressing surprise that I have not been tempted by Caroline's portion into paying my addresses to her!"

"Eh?" Lord Pendril exclaimed unguardedly. Patty flashed him a warning look and he recollected the revelations of the previous day. "Oh, yes! Nice enough girl, but I've no mind to get leg-shackled myself. I daresay he feels the same way," he explained kindly to Vanessa. Patty sent him another look calculated to pin him to his saddle, and he added hastily, "What I mean is, Quentin's not the sort to . . . he's waiting for the right girl—often said so!" he ended lamely.

"Just so," Mr. Travers agreed. Helen gave a quick

involuntary glance in his direction and he met her eyes and smiled warmly, both of them recalling the occasion when he had asked her if she knew Vanessa's sentiments. She turned away again almost at once, and to Lord Pendril said, "I am sure neither of you would be influenced by pecuniary considerations."

Lord Pendril shook his head, but his remark about her extravagance still rankling, Patty said waspishly, "Oh, wouldn't he! The last time the bailiffs got in he was going to offer for the Needham girl!"

"Damn it all! They'd seized my chestnuts!" Lord Pendril protested. "Finest pair of horses I ever owned and they'd have gone to pay off a pack of rascally tradesmen! Be reasonable, my dear girl! Besides, when it came to the point I couldn't bring myself to do it. Too much of a sacrifice. She'd been on the marriage market for three years—got a beam as broad as Henry Watson's best hunter!" He saw Helen was looking bewildered, and in explanation said, "Big fellow—rides about seventeen stone! I keep forgetting you've never been to town. Anyway in the end I didn't need to because Qu . . . I managed to borrow the ready," he corrected hurriedly.

Mr. Travers tensed, but neither Helen nor Vanessa appeared to have noticed the slip. Helen was again talking to Lord Pendril, and the lane now being broadened by grass verges, Patty rode alongside Vanessa. They discussed Brighton for a while, and Patty expressed a longing for a cool sea breeze, but though it was a topic that should have interested Vanessa, Mr. Travers thought she was uneasy, and half her attention, he suspected, was on Helen, by now deep in conversation with the viscount. Several times Vanessa leaned forward and addressed a remark to her in an attempt to draw her into their own discussion, but inexplicably, on each occasion Patty foiled her efforts. After a while he became certain that her interventions were deliberate, and also, by Vanessa's heightened color, giving rise to annoyance. He could not fathom the motives of either of them, and when they returned to the Angel, his curiosity thoroughly aroused, he waylaid Patty in the courtyard.

But to all his questions she would only shake her head, and reply that some things were best left unsaid, and when he persisted, placed a finger against her nose in a knowing and highly ungenteel gesture that in no way decreased his puzzlement.

Chapter Eight

The day by this time was extremely hot without the breeze that had earlier made it supportable, and though she tried to hide it, it was plain that Helen was fatigued. In a worry in case the ride had over-exerted her too soon after her illness, Vanessa bore her off to their bedchamber as soon as their horses had been taken from them. Patty also retired to rest, the effort of being up and dressed for a quarter after ten having begun to take its toll. Lord Pendril, on the other hand, responding to the beneficial effects of country air and regular hours, took the terriers for a run, while Mr. Travers tooled the bays around the lanes to rid them of the excess of energy that was the automatic result of a day in the stable.

All the parties, by chance, met again in the middle of the afternoon when Mr. Travers and Lord Pendril adjourned to the tap to ease their dry and dusty throats. They had only been there a short while, when unknown to them Patty returned from taking Jason for a walk, and in the manner of a reunion, there was almost a repetition of the poodle's introduction to the inn. Barnaby and Patch, settled in a pleasantly somnolent attitude across Lord Pendril's feet, were just drifting off to a dreamland inhabited exclusively by felines and rats when the voice of their archenemy pierced their semiconsciousness. In one movement they were awake and halfway to the door, but Lord Pendril, for once reacting with equal swiftness, roared, "Stay!" at the top of his powerful voice. Since he reinforced the command by hurling his hat at them they froze to the ground, then crept back to his feet to assure him that they had acted before they had had time to recollect themselves.

Lord Pendril, surveying the damage to his previously imaculate beaver, for a while was not disposed to accept their excuses, and this put Patty so much in accord with him that she dispatched Jason upstairs with Bess and came to join them in the tap.

Pausing to refresh herself from Lord Pendril's tankard, she said, "The girls are in the coffee room—they've just come down, and if you've nothing better than this to do, you can take us all to the fair!"

"Eh!" Lord Pendril exclaimed. "What fair?"

"Down on the village green! I couldn't go near because I'd got Jason with me, but they've got sword swallowers and sideshows and all manner of things! In case you'd forgotten, it's Midsummer's Day!"

"I'm dashed sure you'd forgotten as well until you got down there!" Lord Pendril retorted, attempting to rescue his tankard from her grasp. "Give it back to me, Patty! Let me tell you respectable females don't drink ale in the tap!"

She grinned but relinquished it. "Well? Are you going to take us?"

Mr. Travers was about to point out that to deliberately venture into a crowd that would contain a large proportion of his own tenants would be an act of madness on his part, when to his alarm, Vanessa and Helen peeped around the door.

"I thought I heard voices," Vanessa said. "Has Patty told you? There's a fair in the village!"

"Yes," Mr. Travers replied. "But it will draw all the riffraff from miles around. I don't think it is the sort of thing you would care for."

His dampening tone had its effect on Helen, and she said, "Mr. Travers is right, Vanessa. You know Mama would never permit us to go to even the little fair at home."

"Yes, but that was amongst our own people!" Vanessa said impatiently. "There won't be anyone here to report back to the squire's wife!" While Mr. Travers sat thinking that there would be a good many people to report back to his stepmother, she added, "I think it would be an adventure, and if Mr. Travers and Lord Pendril escort us we won't be subjected to any annoyance. "We could put on our simplest dresses and I daresay no one will think us anything out of the way."

It was Mr. Travers's considered opinion that even if she wore an apron and tied a shawl over her head, the sight of her on his arm would arouse more interest in Priors Cross than a visit by the Princess of Wales. The news that Mr. Travers from up at the Court had taken a young woman of quality to the Midsummer Fair would travel across the countryside like wildfire.

He could only pin his hopes on Lord Pendril's aversion to the scheme. His lordship was objecting ener-

getically, but in the face of Patty's determination Mr.
Travers felt it was only a matter of time before he
weakened. When he unwisely lapsed into silence and
allowed Patty to get her word in, she told him roundly
that he could take that hard-done-by expression off
his face and think of her entertainment for a change.
"For I'll tell you now," she concluded, "this last week
hasn't been what I expected, not by any means!"

Roused, Lord Pendril replied that it hadn't been
what he'd had in mind either, but was fortunately recalled to a sense of his company by the sight of Mrs.
Moorcroft's inquisitive features peering into the taproom. From her tightened lips it could be seen that
she held the view that females being present in the
tap was only one degree less discreditable than their
receiving gentlemen in their bedchamber, and on Mr.
Travers very civilly wishing her good afternoon she
withdrew in outrage, presumably to inform her faith-
ful companion of this latest example of depravity.

The terriers, by now having recovered their spirits,
rushed into the hall to encourage her up the stairs,
and their growls, punctuated by little shrieks of fright,
caused Vanessa to dissolve into a helpless fit of gig-
gles.

Resignedly, Lord Pendral said, "What odds will you
lay me that she goes straight to Roberts and tells him
I set 'em on to her!" Somewhat unjustly, he added to
Patty, "It's your fault! You might have known you'd
bring her out on us coming in here!"

"Best part of the time it's the only place I can find
you!" Patty retorted, stung. "That's if you're in at all!"
She started to detail the rest of his shortcomings but
recollected that he had not yet agreed to take her to
the fair and he was quite likely to seize on such a tri-

fling cause as a disagreement to defect. Swallowing her wrath, she said more moderately, "Well, never mind that! Do we poor females have to get on your knees and beg for your company this afternoon? Because there are one or two others who might be glad to take your place!"

Correctly divining this to refer to two middle-aged gentlemen who had arrived that morning and displayed an overt appreciation of Patty's arresting appearance, Lord Pendril regarded her with a martial light in his eye. "If that's the case, my girl, they're welcome! They can pay your shot here as well!"

Patty perceived that she had erred. She hastened to soothe him, while Vanessa told him she had no notion he could be so disobliging. Between them he capitulated and went to shut up Barnaby and Patch while the ladies changed into their most modest gowns. Patty's proved to be of a clear yellow, and when she unfurled a pagoda-shaped parasol in a matching shade, Mr. Travers's faint hopes of melting into the crowd faded entirely. She reminded him forcibly of a large, upturned daffodil, and even a serving maid stopped to watch in round-eyed wonder as they crossed the hall.

But when they reached the fair, it would have been hard to say which of them drew the most eyes. Certainly the first startled glances were usually directed at Patty's ensemble, but Mr. Travers, with quiet resignation, noticed the awe changed to astonishment when they were transferred to himself. Those who realized that the two remarkably lovely young women on each side were of his own social station cast wondering looks after him as they passed, but worst of all were the village matrons who had known him from a boy. It had naturally spread through his servants and their dependents that Mrs. Travers was anxious to see her stepson married and provided with an heir, and to a woman the village dames shared her ambition.

Mr. Travers, confronted at every hand by smiling nods of approval, wondered how long it would be before Vanessa began to query the warmth and respect with which he was constantly greeted.

Fortunately, for the moment they were too taken up with the wonders revealed to them at every turn. They gazed in fascination at the men on stilts and the jugglers, and though Helen was forced to turn her eyes away, Vanessa spent some minutes watching the knife thrower in mute but enjoyable apprehension. All three ladies, however, were suitably impressed by a sideshow depicting the great and glorious victory at Trafalgar, which had taken place the previous autumn, and which was stirringly represented against several remarkably lifelike backdrops. Indeed, the whole thing was so realistic that they emerged more than a little depressed by Nelson's heroic end, and Patty astonished Lord Pendril by saying she thought the spectacle ought to be available for everyone to see as it gave a much better insight into this historic event than was obtainable from the newspapers. Luckily, he was rendered so speechless that he could utter nothing to cause disharmony, and by the time he recovered his voice their attention had been taken by something else.

Neither the bearded lady nor the fattest man in the world appealed to them overmuch and they only paused briefly by these attractions. The sword swallower they would also have passed with averted gaze if it had not been for Mr. Travers and Lord Pendril, who wanted to know how the remarkable feat was achieved. They questioned the man after his performance and were surprised to learn that it was a skill that could be acquired by anyone, provided they were prepared to endure a sore throat for three months or so.

Lord Pendril, tapping the sword and testing its edge with the flat of his thumb, said it looked as though it would reach down clear into a fellow's stomach and he'd be damned if he'd do it.

"You starts off with something smaller like a dagger," the man informed him. "And practices!"

"But do you never cut yourself?" Vanessa inquired, wide-eyed.

"Ain't never done it yet, lady!" the man said, exhibiting his throat. He grinned at her expression. "Though in case you're thinking of trying, it's best to start with a knife that ain't too sharp!" Helen shuddered and he said, "It's not dangerous, not so long as you're careful. Meself, I wouldn't swap with him over there!" He jerked his head to indicate a lad balanced on his hands on top of a long pole that another man was holding aloft. "Now you do get some accidents with that!"

As they watched, the boy at the top removed a hand so that he was balanced on only one, and Helen said fearfully, "If he should fall that distance . . ."

The sword swallower regarded her with benevolent contempt. "It's not him as has to worry, lady—it's the feller *holding* the pole! Crushes his ribs if it falls his way! If I had a son, which I haven't, being cursed with three daughters—begging your pardon—I'd bring him up to follow my own line of business without a worry, but that . . ." He sucked in his breath expressively and shook his head. "There's too many of them never manage to make old bones!"

There was a short silence while everyone dwelt on the frequently sad end of pole balancers, then Lord Pendril said, "Yes—well, very interesting, but there's no need to be cast into a gloom! Came here to enjoy ourselves!" He led the way past where the company were being exhorted to guess the weight of a pig or try the vendor's fresh-baked gingerbread. "Any of you girls want to go in there to see the play?"

Vanessa said the heat inside would probably be unendurable, but they nevertheless halted to read the notices, while Mr. Travers, who had paused to bestow a coin on the sword swallower, cast his eyes around to see if there was any refreshment available.

He failed to discover anything suitable, but as he scanned the booths, his astounded gaze fell on the figure of the one person from whom he had judged himself safe. A little apart from the main crowd and also examining it keenly stood his stepmother. Her head was turning toward him and he let out an oath as he realized that momentarily he was in the middle of a clear space. He could only pray that her eyesight was not sufficiently good to recognize him at such a distance, but another second and a militant expression appeared on her face. Mr. Travers's heart sank into his admirable boots but the instinct for survival was strong. Lord Pendril and the girls had their backs to him, still reading the advertisement for the play, and though it was impossible for him to escape his stepmother, there was a chance he could draw her away from the others.

Swiftly he started forward to meet her, and saw

with satisfaction that the crowd had closed behind him, screening them from her view.

He thought he could imagine the words burning on her tongue and accordingly steered her to where they could not be so readily overheard, but when they were finally face to face, she told him acidly, "I've much to say to you but it can wait for another time! For the moment you can save me and yourself a great deal of trouble by telling me where Charles is!"

"Charles?" Mr. Travers repeated, mystified.

"Yes, Charles! After your conduct this last week, nothing you do can have the power to surprise me, but from the length of time he has spent under my roof these last few years, I expected better of Charles than to be so lost to all sense of propriety as to bring my daughter to the Midsummer Fair! I have ignored his reputation because in spite of it I still believed him to be a gentleman, but I am deeply disappointed. He has betrayed my trust!"

More perplexed than ever, Mr. Travers said, "But Caroline is not with Charles!"

"I would prefer to hear the words from his own mouth!"

"I can assure you, ma'am, that it is quite unnecessary! He is certainly here—he came with me, but there was never any suggestion that Caroline might accompany us! I have no more idea of her whereabouts than you!"

She stared at him, suddenly at a loss. "Don't tell me Caroline has not been coming into the village these last few days on purpose to see him, for I discovered it this morning! What everyone else must think of such forward behavior I can only guess, but she will very soon learn my opinion of it!" Remembering this was not the point at issue, she said, "But if she is not with him now . . ."

"Perhaps, ma'am, you will tell me what made you think she was!"

She gave him a fulminating look. "A very underbred woman at the Angel told me!"

"Mrs. Moorcroft," Mr. Travers murmured. Meeting his stepmother's eye, he said, "You may take it from me that her information in this instance is quite incorrect!"

"Then I cannot understand it! I know Caroline *has* been coming down to the inn, and masquerading under the name of Harmer, though why she should do so I cannot imagine, when everyone here knows her!" She paused for enlightenment, but when Mr. Travers reprehensibly failed to offer it, she went on tartly, "Very well, *don't* tell me, but you may explain what Caroline's horse is doing in the stable there, together with your own horses and Charles's carriage pair, I may add which Roberts was foolish enough to think I might not recognize! That woman—whatever her name may be—told me you had all come to the fair, so I naturally presumed Caroline . . ." She drew a deep breath in gathering wrath. "Let me but get my hands on that tiresome girl! I'll lay my life she is here somewhere, and if she has come alone . . ."

She clucked fretfully, her anger giving way to concern as she thought of her daughter unescorted in such a press of people, and with sudden inspiration Mr. Travers asked, "Was there a big, dark brown horse in the stable with Caroline's mare?"

Irritably, she said, "I believe there was, but what has that to do with the matter, pray?"

"Everything, ma'am. Wherever she may be, young William Challiner is with her!"

"William!"

He nodded, and in more mollified tones, she said, "I fail to see why he could not call at the Court in a proper manner, but if you are sure Caroline is in his company, then my mind is relieved! I shall have a word with him, however! I should have thought he would know better than to be taking off a girl of seventeen without her mother's permission, and not even a groom in attendance!"

Mr. Travers grinned. "When I saw him last, his intentions were everything of the most correct! I think it is your daughter, ma'am, who is to blame!"

Essentially a just woman, Mrs. Travers acknowledged the truth of this, and he added, "William seems much struck with her, and she is certainly not averse to him!" He hesitated, to allow her to digest the idea, then said, "Perhaps they will make a match of it!"

For a moment she was taken aback. "Caroline is far too young . . ."

"She will be eighteen in less than six months time," Mr. Travers interrupted. "And though you may consider her too young for marriage, *she* has thought of little else for the past year!"

"Well—it would not be a brilliant match, but I should have no objection. I have always found William an extremely pleasant young man, and I hope I have too much sense to place worldly advancement above worth of character and a comfortable situation. She can only just have met him again, of course, for he has been away, so it is early days to be making plans, but yes, I think it would do very well! Provided Caroline's escapades don't come to Lady Challiner's ears, for then *she* might have something to say to it and I couldn't find it in my heart to blame her!"

"Quite so, ma'am," Mr. Travers said meekly.

Her immediate concern for her daughter abated, Mrs. Travers eyed him frostily. "Which brings me to you! Never have I been more embarrassed! I could forgive you if you had decided to stay on with your friends a little longer, but you have been a week at the Angel, and please don't insult me by trying to convince me otherwise! You must have been perfectly well aware that Elizabeth was at the Court, and yet you stayed away! Heaven knows I have no wish to persuade you into marriage with a girl not agreeable to you, but for you to refuse even to meet her when she had been invited! It was discourteous in the extreme! If you have no consideration for Elizabeth's feelings, you might at least think of mine!"

"I fear," Mr. Travers said apologetically, "that on the subject of my prospective bride, we shall never agree!"

"I wish you will rid yourself of this foolish notion that their motives are purely mercenary in every case!"

As Mr. Travers permitted himself a disbelieving smile, she said sharply, "I did not say it did not weigh with them at all! We are all but human after all, and a man of your means must resign himself to it! I tell you now you will not find a girl who is not influenced by it!"

"Won't I?" Mr. Travers queried. "But I think I *have* found one, ma'am!"

For a moment the sense of his words seemed not to penetrate. "*What* did you say?" she inquired faintly.

"I have discovered a girl who is not in the least influenced by my possessions."

"I don't believe it!" Mrs. Travers stated, her voice still feeble. "After all these years of my trying . . . Take me out of this crowd! I cannot think with such a noise going on!"

Obediently, Mr. Travers led her through the caravans to the outskirts of the fair. In the interlude she had time to examine the implications of his startling disclosure and came to the conclusion that he must be contemplating a misalliance. Turning to face him she said resolutely, "You cannot have met her in the ordinary way without my hearing of it, so you may as well tell me at once who she is!"

"Her name is Vanessa Hartland," Mr. Travers told her equably, ignoring the slighting imputation.

She looked at him sharply. "One of the Yorkshire Hartlands?"

"She is related, but only distantly." As Mrs. Travers still appeared doubtful, he said, "Her family was impoverished, but you need not fear for her breeding, ma'am."

"If she is of good family, I have nothing to say against it. You, above all people, have no need to consider her portion! But how you can stand there and tell me a penniless girl can have no interest in your circumstances I do not know!"

"That is easily explained. I have not told her of them!"

For the second time, she stared at him speechless. Finally, she said, "You have not told her . . . ! Then you are not yet betrothed! Nothing is settled!"

"Not so far," Mr. Travers admitted. "I am not even sure she will take me."

Bluntly, she demanded, "Quentin, are you in love with this girl?"

He nodded, and she declared, "I was right when I said you were incapable of managing your own affairs! I would not have believed that a man of your age could go about the business in such a ridiculous fashion. I presume that for some reason she is staying in the village? Then bring her up to the Court tomorrow morning and we will get the affair resolved!"

Mr. Travers cringed inwardly, but since he had not the smallest intention of falling in with this scheme, he merely said, "Very well, ma'am."

"I shall expect you both about eleven o'clock then! We will make it a strictly informal visit—it is easier to form impressions!"

A slightly steely light appeared in Mr. Travers's eyes. "I am afraid that your impressions hold no interest for me. My own mind is made up, whatever they may be!"

Far from showing resentment at this, she gave a brisk nod of approval. "I have hopes for you at last! Now you may take me back to my carriage. I daresay the sight of us together in this place will give the villagers a topic of conversation for weeks!" She looked down her nose distastefully at the multitude swarming around the various amusements. "If you do encounter Caroline, send her home to me at once, though I am sure William has too much sense of duty to bring her here!"

Mr. Travers could not share her hopes though he refrained from saying so. He escorted her to where her barouche was drawn up on to the grass beside the road and thankfully saw her pointed in the direction of home. Returning to the fair, he was in some doubt as to his ability to find the others again in the crowd, but he sighted them almost at once on the fringe of the circle of caravans. If they had been there more than a few moments they must have seen him with his stepmother, and Vanessa's first words provided the confirmation.

Reproachfully, she said, "We have been looking for you all over, and now we find you were lured from our side and have been bestowing your attentions on another female! Shame on you!"

"Not lured, but snatched!" he told her with a grin. "That was Caroline's mother. Apparently the wretched girl has slipped off again and Mrs. Harmer feared she had come to the fair on her own and was naturally very disturbed."

"Would she do such a thing?" Vanessa queried.

"Very likely," he said cheerfully. "But in this instance I believe she is with young William Challiner so she cannot come to any harm, though she will undoubtedly get a severe scolding when she gets home." His eyes scanned Helen's face quickly. "Have you ladies exhausted your energies in my absence? I think we should find somewhere to sit down!"

"I am not tired, sir," Helen averred quickly.

Lord Pendril said, "Well, I am, and devilish hot too! I vote we find somewhere where you girls can rest and I can get a tankard of ale!"

The hostelry on the village green, though inferior to the Angel, was clean and respectable, and confident of his ability to procure a quiet room, Mr. Travers suggested that they should repair thither to recoup their strength for the walk back to the inn. The heat by now was oppressive, the air heavy and sultry, and the ladies sank down thankfully on the rather hard wooden chairs in the Lion's back parlor. Patty, unrestrained by the conventions obtaining in polite society, immediately removed her sandals and spread her toes blissfully on the cold stone quarries underfoot, though out of consideration for the finer feelings of the others, Lord Pendril excepted, she consented to tuck them back under her skirt whenever the landlord came into the room. This individual, though flustered by the quality of his customers, produced a tolerable ale for the gentlemen, and after the ladies had quenched their thirst with lemonade, ventured to offer them a wine. Not the one he usually served, he hastened to assure them, which in all honesty he could not recommend, but the one his wife brewed each year, which was always highly praised by several people whose judgment on such matters he valued.

Mr. Travers tasted it distrustfully but to his surprise found it perfectly palatable and filled all their glasses. He saw that it removed some of the tiredness from Helen's face, though she still appeared a little worn, and Patty, glancing at her shrewdly, declared that she could not contemplate putting her feet back in her sandals until the day had cooled.

"And what is more, I'm hungry," she said. "Charles, find out what the landlord can offer us to eat! I don't want anything hot so there ought to be something he can give us!"

Vanessa threw her a grateful glance, and as it turned out the landlord was able to provide an excellent cold veal pie, followed by strawberries and cream, which they all enjoyed.

It was beginning to grow dusk by the time they rose to go back to the Angel and they elected to go the shorter way by the road. Lord Pendril, in a rollicking humor due to the effects of the homemade wine, led the way with Patty and Helen. He occasionally broke into snatches of song, and it was plain he was in an entertaining mood, keeping both ladies in a state of merriment.

Walking behind with Mr. Travers, Vanessa slowed her steps to say shyly, "You are all of you very kind to us, and I do not know how to thank you. Helen is usually so conscious of her limp and the fact that she tires easily, but when she is with you and Lord Pendril and Patty I don't think it crosses her mind! Even when you stayed at the Lion so that she might rest it was so tactfully done that she was not made to feel uncomfortable."

"To tell you the truth, I'd forgotten about her limp," Mr. Travers said. Meeting her surprised gaze, he added, "Oh, I know she has one—I didn't mean that, but being with her so much these last few days I no longer notice it. The reason I thought it advisable for her to rest this afternoon was because I feared she might be overtaxing herself after her bout of asthma. It has been by far the hottest day this year, though I think we may be in for a storm."

He indicated the dark clouds building up in the west, and Vanessa nodded, pulling a wry face. "Isn't it strange? Two weeks of nothing but sunshine and one cannot think of rain."

"We should savor it if it is to be our last fine evening," Mr. Travers said lightly. The distance between themselves and Lord Pendril's group had increased and he slowed his pace still further. Tomorrow would bring his stepmother down on the scene, full of plain speaking and good intentions. As Vanessa gave him a faintly inquiring look, he said, "Let the others hurry if they want to. I have something to say that is not for their ears!"

"Indeed! How very mysterious!"

Her tone was so completely unself-conscious that he realized she could have no inkling of what he was about to ask her. He knew he was probably being too precipitate, but the balmy summer evening decided him.

"Miss Vanessa, it is hardly a week since you and your sister arrived here, so perhaps what I am about to say will come as a surprise, but we have been so constantly together that it feels like a much longer acquaintanceship."

He looked down at her, and a little breathlessly she said, "I . . . Helen and I have felt the same way, sir."

"Then it will not come as such a surprise!" He paused and turned her gently to face him. "I can perhaps hope that you are also not unaware of the great regard I have for you."

In the twilight she gazed at him dumbly and he took both her hands and held them in his own. "I realize that you know little of me and I may be a fool to put the question so early, but I have no doubt of my own feelings." She still did not speak and he pressed her nerveless fingers. "I am asking you to marry me, Vanessa!"

Chapter Nine

She stood frozen, conscious only of the throb of her pulse in her ears. He was asking *her* to marry him! For a moment she allowed herself to admit that it was what she wished for above all else in the world—that she had known it almost from the first day of meeting him; then she had a picture of Helen's stricken eyes if she told her she was going to marry Mr. Travers, and she knew it was impossible. No matter that she had been wrong when she believed him to be in love with Helen and there was no hope of her sister winning him, still she could not administer such a blow.

"Vanessa?" he questioned gently.

She shook her head at him, desperately forcing back tears. "Mr. Travers, I am sorry, but the answer must be no! Forgive me, but I had no idea . . ." Unable to go on, she stopped and took a deep breath. "If I have encouraged you to think . . . to think my answer would be otherwise, I do most sincerely beg your pardon!"

"It is no fault of yours if I have been mistaken!" He was still holding her hands but she withdrew them now and he looked at her searchingly. "Was I mistaken? I don't mean to press you for your reasons if you don't wish it, but we have dealt so extremely together. . . . I hope I don't make myself appear conceited, but is there some objection I know nothing of, which could perhaps be overcome?"

Swallowing, she said, "No, nothing like that, Mr. Travers."

"Is it because of Helen?"

Her eyes flew to his face. "Because of Helen?" she repeated. "How . . . in what way?"

"If you are worried about her future, you must know that she could make her home with us for as long as she wished. I hold her in considerable affection in her own right, while you would be pleased to still have her companionship and it would ease your mind to be able to watch over her in case of illness."

Wordlessly, Vanessa stared up at him. What he had outlined was all she needed for complete happiness. But for Helen to live day after day in the same house as the man she loved and that man married to her sister? It was unthinkable.

Summoning every ounce of resolution she possessed, she said, "This is another instance of your true kindness, Mr. Travers, and . . . and I appreciate it very much, but my answer must still be no. Your friendship I value greatly, but marriage requires stronger feelings and it would be wrong of me to agree to marry you when I lack them." Miraculously her voice held steady but she knew if she looked at him he would recognize it for a lie. She stared fixedly at her clasped hands, so lost in misery that his next words barely affected her.

An edge in his voice, he said slowly, "Then it is to be hoped you can summon them for your merchant!"

Even as her lips framed a hot denial it came to her that this was the easiest solution, and she kept silent. At least if he believed her to be so mercenary he would be able to congratulate himself on his escape.

But it was all she could do not to cry out when he said, "I see. I trust you will not be disappointed."

Raising her eyes at last, she retorted, "At least you cannot accuse me of hiding my intentions, Mr. Travers—I believe I said as much to you on our first meeting! Nor do I think I am singular in my ambition. Even in such rural seclusion as I come from, it is known that a woman will never lack for suitors if she has fifty thousand pounds to recommend her, and a man of fortune may almost pick and choose for a bride! To gain their object they will all pretend a regard they do not feel and be congratulated by their friends on it, so why should you censure me!"

"It is not so much censure as regret. I remember very well what you said that time. Can you tell me my reply?"

"That there are other things in life besides money!" Her throat was tight with holding back her tears, both for what she was giving up and what he must think of her. "But it is not money, but security and freedom from worry for the future!" She was quoting now from what she had believed at the time. He had changed her views and she would have been happy now to share her life with him under any circumstances, but the readiness of the words convinced him that she was speaking the truth.

His face expressionless, he said, "I can only say I am sorry you feel the way you do."

She bowed her head and, turning, started to walk after the others, by now invisible in the gloom. They were both silent, in part because there seemed nothing more to say, and because their own thoughts occupied them to the exclusion of all else. Vanessa's at first were concentrated on her own misery, then the wider implications began to occur to her. They would have to move on at once. A few short days ago when they had set out on their journey she had been nervous but exhilarated, looking forward to her first view of the sea and excited by the prospect of spending the summer in Brighton. Now the same future seemed joyless and drear and she wished with all her heart that they had never made that fatal stop at the Angel. It was not true that what one never had one never missed—it was possible to wish for something desperately that had always been out of reach, but to have a dream placed squarely in front of one and be forced to reject it was surely the cruelest deprivation of all. Hard on these bitter thoughts came the realization that she must make up some excuse to Helen for leaving, and her sister's unhappiness would be no less than her own. In spite of all efforts the tears welled up in her eyes and she was grateful for the dark that hid them from Mr. Travers. She would have to say something to Helen as soon as she got in, and try as she might, she could only think of one reason, and that would mean Helen's opinion of Mr. Travers would be every bit as low as his was of herself. That they would not even have kindly memories of each other seemed somehow to make the situation worse and a feeling of disgust built up in her for what she was about to do.

She parted from Mr. Travers in the entrance hall of the Angel. He gave her only a quiet "Good night," which she told herself he could not be blamed for after what she had done, but it was in such marked contrast to previous evenings when they had lingered to talk that the ache in her throat started afresh. Holding herself rigidly she mounted the stairs, but once inside the room her command slipped and she sat on the bed, the tears sliding down her face. She could only shake her head to Helen's questions, but finally she recovered some measure of control, and nerved herself to tell her what she felt must surely be the blackest, most dastardly lie every uttered.

Helen, acutely distressed, was still asking her what had happened to upset her so, and forcing herself to speak calmly, she said, "It was Mr. Travers. Mrs. Moorcroft was right, and so were we in what we first thought. On the way back here, he . . . he put a proposition to me, and . . . and it was something of a shock, that is all."

She expected Helen to be completely overcome, but though she paled, she betrayed none of the emotion Vanessa had prepared herself for, and incredibly her chief concern seemed to be for Vanessa herself.

For a moment she cradled her head against her, then said, "Do not think of it. I have been a little foolish too, and when one is foolish one must expect . . . disappointments. We will leave here tomorrow. It will be best for both of us."

Vanessa stared at her, troubled by her unnatural calmness, and Helen smiled slightly. "There is nothing to stay for after all. It is true that I have stupidly let myself indulge in hopes, but I knew I was deluding myself, and what you have told me is only confirmation."

Her quiet dignity made Vanessa ashamed of the upheaval inside her and she determined to show the same strength. Only in fiction did people die of broken hearts or go into declines, and she was made of sterner stuff.

Resolutely she tucked her handkerchief back into her pocket. "I seem to be becoming most undesirably lachrymose, which will never do! Shall we put some of our things in tonight to save time in the morning?"

"We could perhaps try to get seats on the Mail tomorrow," Helen suggested tentatively.

Vanessa agreed, hiding her surprise. Though the coach had been half empty for much of the journey from Shifnall, she doubted their being able to obtain two inside seats, and in spite of the fact that it halted in Daventry for breakfast, it would mean getting there for six o'clock at the latest. They could but try, however. At least the early start would prevent a meeting with Mr. Travers and if they did manage to book seats, they would not have to stay a day and a night in the town in order to catch it the next morning. She found she was torn between the desire to see Mr. Travers just once more before they went, and a dread of seeing what must surely be contempt in his eyes as they rested on her. But the reflection that Helen must be suffering the same indecision stiffened her, and like the repetition of a dream, she once more collected up their things and packed them in the trunk. Neither of them spoke of the possibility of another attack of asthma interfering with their plans. As always, Vanessa put the medicines in the trunk last, but she felt it would be tempting providence to so much as mention them.

They talked only of trivial things as they put their traveling clothes out ready for the early departure, and when there was no more to be done, Vanessa went to settle their bill, Helen accompanying her in order to say good-bye to Barnaby and Patch. There would be no time the following morning.

This time Roberts was prepared for their request for a post chaise. From the demeanor of Mr. Travers, who was nearing the end of his second bottle of Burgundy in the private parlor, he had guessed that something was seriously amiss, and though not a sentimental man, he was distressed at the way things had fallen out. When Helen asked if he would get the terriers, he was conscious of a most unaccustomed lump in his throat. She bent to give them each a farewell pat, and without regard for what would be the feelings of Lord Pendril, he said suddenly:

"Miss, you can have them if you want!"

Her eyes still on them, Helen smiled faintly, shaking her head. "I could not take them with me, and besides . . ." She did not finish the sentence, but Roberts knew she was thinking of their attachment to Lord Pendril, and the lump threatened to obstruct his throat entirely.

He cleared it, saying gruffly, "Well, a pleasant journey to you, ladies, and I'll have the chaise at the door not a minute later than five!" With forced jocularity, he added, "Take care not to get near my old parrot again!" but neither of them could manage a smile. Remembering Mr. Travers's aspect when he had last seen him, he thought it would be hard to decide which of the parties was the most dismal. As a matter of duty he went to inform him of what was going on, but without any real hope of being attended to. Much to his surprise he found him still what he would term sober, but he evinced no interest in the news, and shaking his head, Roberts descended to the cellar to fetch up a third bottle of wine. Mr. Travers, he knew, was no tippler but a man who appreciated a good wine, and in his present mood he barely tasted let along appreciated the qualities of his finest Burgundy. It was a sad business altogether, and Roberts found himself almost hoping for another mishap like the one that had prevented the Misses Hartland's departure on the previous occasion.

But nothing occurred to hinder it. When he served them with coffee just before five they were both a little pale, but Helen's breathing was as regular as his own. With a feeling of helplessness he closed the door of the chaise ten minutes later and watched from the road until they were borne out of sight.

Inside the carriage, Vanessa sat with her eyes fixed blindly on the figure of the postilion. There was no other solution, she knew, but the one she was taking; yet as a condemned man will trust to the last that something unforseen will avert the inevitable end, so she had gone to bed with that tiny glimmer of hope. But no miracle occurred in the night and now her unwilling feet had brought her up into the chaise and every minute carried her farther and farther away from the man she loved.

It seemed fitting that when they were put down in Daventry the sun should have disappeared behind sullen gray clouds. It had shone on them all the time they were in Priors Cross. During all the walks and rides with Mr. Travers, nothing more ominous had appeared in the sky than wisps like cotton wool, but as she stood paying off the postboy, thunder rolled, and heavy, widely spaced drops heralded the storm that was to come. She needed nothing else to complete her sense of utter desolation.

The fates that had conspired to block their progress on that previous departure seemed now to exert themselves to aid them. At the coach office she was told there were two seats on the Mail as far as Stoney Stratford, where they would be able to catch the up Mail from Birmingham.

By the time they had purchased their tickets and seen the trunk taken safely onto the coach, it was raining in earnest, and they joined the other two travelers who were breakfasting in the coffee room of the inn. Nauseated by the smell of greasy eggs, however, they very soon returned to the coach to take their seats. Damp and chilled, they settled themselves in, but when their fellow passengers arrived, it transpired that they were in the places the other two ladies had been occupying since Shrewsbury, and to which they considered they had an inalienable right, and though Vanessa and Helen quickly apologized and moved over, it was apparent they were offended.

It was an inauspicious start to an exhausting and miserable journey, during which the rain continued unabated from a leaden sky. The inside of the coach smelled unpleasantly of wet wool and the previous occupants, and before they were halfway to their destination they were stiff and cramped, and Vanessa would gladly have partaken of the eggs that had so revolted her at Daventry. Neither of the other two passengers addresssed a single remark either to each other or to them, and in consequence, she and Helen found they were conducting their own conversation in whispers. If the other two women had been agreeable, she would have welcomed some information and advice from them. The nearer they got to London the more nervous she became, and what had seemed an adventure when they started out from home was becoming a continual anxiety. She had no idea where they were to stay when they reached town, and remembering that the squire's wife had told her the prices in all the hotels were shockingly high, she worried in case she had not sufficient money with her to meet their expenses. Merely to have a decent inn recommended to them would have been a great relief, a brief perusal of *The Traveler's Guide* having supplied her with nothing more helpful than the conviction that where they escaped extortion amounting to robbery, they were likely to be submitted to damp sheets and various other evils that the author could not bring himself to describe even in euphemisms.

The only comfort was that though she strained her ears with listening for it over the rumble of the wheels, there was no sign of one of Helen's dreaded attacks. Indeed, when they finally got down at Stoney Stratford, Vanessa thought her own case might be the worse, for she had begun to feel more than a little travel sick.

In any event, she had ample time to recover. They had over three hours to wait before the Birmingham to London Mail came through, and in spite of what she had been told, when it arrived it was full. Near to tears she went back to the booking office to be told that the Liverpool up Mail would be coming through later. Unfortunately, as a totally inexperienced traveler she did not think to inquire what time it arrived in London. Consequently, it was when they were nearly dead from fatigue and long past any coherent thought that they found themselves at their journey's end. It was half past four in the morning, black and wet, and never had Vanessa's spirits been at a lower ebb. They were put down at the Swan with Two Necks, which was larger than any inn she had seen in her life before, but if it took every penny in her possession she could not have considered moving from it. Shown to a room, they both lay on top of the bed, thankful to be released at last from the swaying and jolting, and slept until ten o'clock.

They awoke, feeling grubby and travel stained, to wonder how they could have remained unconscious of the noise and shouting. The Angel, which at first had seemed to be noisy, was by comparison a haven of peace, and Vanessa sat up with her head already throbbing. She was astonished to think she could have slept in her clothes and wanted nothing so much as a wash, but was almost too apprehensive in such surroundings to ring the bell for water.

Telling herself not to be ridiculous she nerved herself to give the bell rope a tug, and on observing the quality of the chambermaid who presently answered it, recovered her composure enough to request that their dresses, crumpled from the packing, should be pressed. Neither she nor Helen felt confident enough to go downstairs for breakfast until this task had been carried out, and they sat by the window, listening and watching, while they waited for their clothes to be returned.

The courtyard, wet and muddy, was alive with all manner of persons, some with legitimate business there, and some selling pies and fruit and bootlaces.

Their accents were harsh and almost incomprehensible to those unused to their nasal tones, and after a while, Vanessa found her tired mind drifting. It returned, as it had done during all those weary miles in the coach, to Mr. Travers.

She must have sighed, for she found Helen had withdrawn her gaze from the scene below them and was watching her.

Vanessa smiled tremulously. "Why, oh why did you ever let me persuade you into leaving our home?"

Seriously, Helen said, "Because I knew in my heart that you were right. We could not continue as we were! I own I was frightened at the prospect of leaving and I was nervous during the journey, but we are actually here in London in spite of everything."

Vanessa shuddered. "I should not care to do it again!"

"It would not have been troublesome if it had not been for my stupid illness. We should have come straight here on the one coach."

"Yes, but you are not to be blaming yourself for something you could not help." Her eyes returned to the courtyard, gray and dirty in the rain. At the Angel they had looked out over the big, old fruit trees in the orchard, and beyond them to the fields and the river. And Mr. Travers had been at the Angel, smoothing their path when they arrived, getting Roberts to change their room, putting his own private parlor at their disposal. With him to protect them, they had known nothing of the difficulties usually experienced by young women traveling alone. She recalled the inn where they had dined at Stoney Stratford. The waiter had been indifferent, serving first those parties who were accompanied by a man, and the food when it arrived was not what they had ordered. When she pointed this out he had been disposed to argue, and by that time she had been so worn down that she had flinched from drawing attention to herself by insisting that he change it.

And London, which she had longed to visit ever since she put up her hair, was drear and wet and smelled of the drains.

As though sharing her thoughts, Helen said, "Could we not go on to Brighton? Unless you wish to look at the shops, but the weather is so bad . . ."

Vanessa shook her head. "I don't feel like it. It would be different if we had someone to take us around and show us the places of interest, but to tell the truth, I think we should only feel ignorant and rather lonely. Brighton is not so very far. We could perhaps come back for a few days when we are more used to finding our way about."

But she didn't want to go to Brighton either. She didn't want to go anywhere except back to tell Mr. Travers that she was not heartless and mercenary; that it had all been lies; and if a hundred rich merchants asked her to marry them she would turn them down without hesitation. But nothing had changed, and she couldn't do it to Helen. She must carry on with her original plan. Perhaps one day, if everything worked out as she hoped, she would be able to go back to Priors Cross and discover his address from Caroline Harmer. She could write to her in any case—there would be nothing wrong in that—tell her she had mislaid his address, and . . . and what? And it would be better if she ceased such foolish imaginings.

She gave herself a mental shake and got up to put her creased redingote back on. "I will find out where the coach goes from and see if I can book our seats. I do not know how long I shall be so don't be supposing that I have been abducted if I am not back immediately."

She tried to make her voice sound more confident than she felt, but outside the door her courage almost deserted her. They had arrived mindless with fatigue and when the corridors were dimly lit, and she had no idea even which way to turn. Fortunately, as she stood there hesitant, a respectable-looking chambermaid came toward her and asked if she could help. With relief, Vanessa realized that she spoke in the soft accents of the country. She confessed that she was lost and wished to book on the Mail for Brighton and had absolutely no idea which way to go. The girl, who was about her own age, volunteered to show her, and on the way pointed out the public rooms where they could get their meals. Thankful to have it all made easy, Vanessa gave her half a crown, trying to remember what amount *The Traveler's Guide* recommended as gratuities for servants. Apparently it was adequate, for the girl took her up to the bedchamber again afterward and she was able to report to Helen that she had successfully accomplished her mission.

After that it was all remarkable simple. They slept a little during the afternoon, dined at six, and eight o'clock found them on the coach again. Their fellow travelers were a husband and wife of comfortable aspect who were able to tell them of small, worrying details such as where to obtain transport when they reached Brighton, and they began to feel more relaxed, and even dozed. They awoke with a jolt, however, when the coach halted at just after one. The couple on the other side still slept soundly, but the passengers on the roof had begun to sing and tap out the time with their feet, and Vanessa realized there was no possibility of her settling back. She found that the resignation with which she had set out on this last stage had deserted her. Then, she had taken herself roundly to task and resolved not to think any more of the future that might have been, but with the lowness of spirits that sometimes comes with the early hours of the morning, she could not prevent her mind from returning to it. She hardly noticed when the coach jerked into motion again, and it was Helen who brought her back to reality.

Under cover of the noise from the wheels, she said, "I know it must be worse for you than for me."

For a moment Vanessa could not think and the words had no meaning for her. She had no doubt that Helen's mind was also back in Priors Cross—she had thought of little else in the past two days and it must be the same for her sister—but she could not make out the sense of the remark.

Sitting up straighter, she said, "I don't understand. Why should it be worse for me?"

Helen's profile was etched against the grayness of the night sky and she saw her shake her head. "It must be, for your own case was quite different. I was so sure, right from the beginning, that one day soon you would come to tell me Mr. Travers had asked you to marry him, whereas for me," she shook her head again in the darkness while Vanessa's mind reeled with shock, "I knew Lord Pendril never thought of me."

Chapter Ten

Mr. Travers, in spite of his resolve to drown his sorrows in Burgundy, went to bed depressingly sober. He then spent some hours in watching the flickering pattern cast on the ceiling by his candle, alternating between a desire to go at once and tell Vanessa that she would be lucky to discover a merchant who exceeded his own wealth, and the determination to allow her to manage her own destiny, which he devoutly hoped she would regret.

He went to sleep decided on the latter course, but awoke at cockcrow with his intentions fixed on the first. He got up and dressed immediately, spent half an hour fidgeting around his room, then unable to stand the inactivity any longer, went downstairs.

Roberts, his countenance lugubrious, was just coming out of the public dining room, but his expression changed to astonishment when Mr. Travers greeted him cheerfully.

"You're more full of pep than I thought you'd be!"

he commented. "Nor I didn't reckon to see you up this early after what you put away last night! I take it you've decided you're best off without the wench!"

"No," Mr. Travers returned, ignoring this unflattering reference to his beloved. "Merely I have reached the conclusion that my case is not, after all, hopeless. I shall let Miss Hartland into my closely guarded secret!"

Roberts's jaw dropped. "But she's gone!"

"Gone!"

"An hour since! I told you last night! She hired a chaise for five o'clock to take them into Daventry! They were catching the Mail there!"

"It seems I was not attending," Mr. Travers said dully. "But if she was so eager to depart it may be for the best."

He turned on his heel and went out through the front door, leaving Roberts to shake his head mournfully after him. Mr. Travers, he thought, was hard hit.

He did not return until midday when he went straight into the tap. Roberts thought of telling him that the shoulders of his coat were soaked through with the rain, but since Mr. Travers could hardly fail to be aware of it, he held his peace and went to draw a tankard of his customary brew.

Mr. Travers, however, shook his head. "I'll have another bottle of the Burgundy," he said, and went to sit by the hearth.

Shrugging, Roberts carried it over. He hovered for a moment in case he wished to unburden his heart, but Mr. Travers only stared silently into the glass, so he withdrew, quietly closing the door.

He was still sitting there when Lord Pendril burst in with Barnaby and Patch, all three of them dripping wet. The terriers shook themselves energetically, splattering the floor with mud and water. They then dashed back to his lordship to tell him how much they had enjoyed the outing, and lay down panting across his feet.

Lord Pendril stirred them with his toe. "Move off, you little devils! How can I get a glass of ale!" With vague surprise he noted that Mr. Travers was drinking wine, but putting it down to the sudden chill in the weather, he said, "Where are the girls? Haven't seen either of 'em this morning!"

Without raising his eyes from the depths of his glass, Mr. Travers replied, "They have left."

"Eh!" In the act of raising the tankard to his lips, Lord Pendril spilled it down his breeches. "What did you say?"

"They have left," Mr. Travers repeated. "They went at just after five this morning."

"But . . ." Lost for words for a moment, Lord Pendril stared at him. "Why would they do a thing like that?"

"I asked Vanessa to marry me last night and she turned me down. One would therefore presume that she wished, at all cost, to avoid any more of my company."

"Turned you down! Why?"

"Why shouldn't she? It is her privilege! She rejected me because she still has an ambition to marry riches! I deliberately misled her about my circumstances so that I could be certain that she was not influenced by them and I have received my answer. Viewed dispassionately, I have no cause for complaint."

For a long while Lord Pendril regarded him silently. Finally he said, "Pass me that bottle!"

There was very little conversation between them during the next hour, and they had just reached the stage where they were inclined to be maudlin when Patty, informed by Roberts that they were bent on drinking themselves to a standstill, flung open the door of the tap.

Arms akimbo she stood surveying them, then demanded, "What's the meaning of this?"

"She turned him down," Lord Pendril volunteered. "They've left!"

"Is that any reason for you to drink yourself stupid at this time of day?"

Lord Pendril looked to her owlishly. "He's a friend of mine!"

"And you're a fool!" Patty informed him. She turned to Mr. Travers. "Why did she turn you down?"

"The obvious inference is that she doesn't love me!"

"If ever I saw such a pair of idiots!" Patty exclaimed, exasperated. "Is that what you believe?"

"Why not, since it is what she told me! She thanked me for my kindnesses, but regretted that I have not enough to offer her. She wants brocade curtains in the kitchen," he added irrelevantly.

"Well, good God, you can afford to give 'em to her! Not but what it's as plain as a pikestaff that that wasn't the true reason!" She bent over Lord Pendril, studying him closely. "And it's no use your trying to convince me that all this is for his sake! It's because the sister had gone as well!"

He squinted up at her. "What?"

Impatiently she seized him by the shoulder and

shook him. "Try to talk some sense! Are you in love with the girl or aren't you?"

"Of course I'm not!" Lord Pendril said, irritable at having his head rocked backward and forward. "Never heard such damned nonsense. . . ." He stopped as the revelation came to him, and looked up at her in dawning wonder. "By Jupiter! You're right!"

"Heaven send me patience! Of course I'm right!" As he still made no move, she gave him another shake. "What are you going to do about it?"

He blinked, fighting against the effects of the Burgundy. "What should I do?"

"Well, you won't accomplish anything sitting there! You'd better get after her!"

It took a moment for the import of her words to sink in. "Go after her . . . of course! They're going to Brighton as well!" He started across the room, knocking over a chair in his haste, but turned back to kiss her soundly. "Patty, you're a girl in a million!"

"Get on with you," Patty said tolerantly. "And mind you don't break your neck in your hurry!"

Kissing her again he went out, Barnaby and Patch at his heels, and Patty sat down in his vacated chair.

Mr. Travers looked at her, a glimmer of amusement in his eyes. "What will you do now you've sent him off, Patty?"

He refilled his glass as he spoke, but she took it out of his hand. "You don't want any more of that!"

Mr. Travers shrugged and she regarded him consideringly. "Never mind about me. I told you before I was thinking about getting married myself and this affair has done no more than make up my mind for me! I don't doubt I shall miss the theatre, but I've a fancy to settle down and have children before I get any older. I'm going back to London, but not to be rattled and jolted all the way as I should be if I went with Charles now. The truth is, he's in no condition to drive and he's likely to overturn." She paused to take a mouthful of his wine. "I think you should take him in your curricle to make sure he comes to no harm."

Mr. Travers looked across at her, suddenly alert. "Are you really worried he might overturn?"

"You can see for yourself he's far from sober!" Meeting his searching gaze, she said, "But apart from that though, I don't pretend to know why Vanessa Hartland told you what she did—but if she didn't spend last night crying her eyes out, I don't know females!"

"Then why did she turn me down?"

"I've told you, I don't know—it's up to you to find out! In my opinion she's head over heels in love with you, but more than that I can't say!"

"Patty, if you're right . . ."

She heaved an exasperated sigh. "You're as bad as Charles! Are you going to sit here talking about it?"

"No," Mr. Travers said, getting to his feet. "I don't know how to thank you, Patty . . ."

"No need," she interrupted. "Come and see me when I'm turned respectable. If you want to do me a service, make sure Charles pays my shot here and arranges with his coachman to get me back to town. The state he's in he's liable to forget."

He lifted her hand to his lips. "I'll see to it, I promise, and I hope you have five children and are happy to the end of your days. Now I must have the bays put to or Charles will be off before me! Good-bye, Patty, and good luck!"

She raised his glass in a salute and he went into the hall where Lord Pendril cannoned into him. "Dear boy! The very one I want! I was thinking! It would be quicker if I took your curricle!"

"Nothing simpler," Mr. Travers told him. "I too am going to Brighton!" Lord Pendril beamed at him and he added, "You are to make arrangements for Patty's transportation home in your own carriage."

"That's the other reason I wanted your curricle! Can't leave poor old Patty stranded! Now, where's Roberts? I want him!"

"He will be relieved to know it," Mr. Travers murmured, aware that his lordship's casual attitude to such things as bills was responsible for some slight unease in Roberts's bosom.

"Yes," Lord Pendril said blithely. "The thing is, I want to buy these two terriers off him!"

Half an hour later they were off, Barnaby and Patch sitting between them as though born to their elevated sphere in life, and Walker standing up at the back. Mr. Travers, by now completely sober, set a brisk pace, and the bays, if anything freshed by the driving rain, stepped out keenly. In Daventry they were assured at the inn that Vanessa and Helen had got on the London Mail, and they set out again, confident, by reason of the fact that Mr. Travers kept fast horses stabled all along the route, of reaching town before them.

They achieved their objective, having passed the coach somewhere along the way, presumably when it halted for a change of team. Mr. Travers paused to inquire at the last turnpike and found that the Mails from Holyhead returned to the Golden Cross Inn at Charing Cross, and thither they repaired. They were chilled and wet, and having stopped only once on the road for a piece of cold pie that they ate standing, they were both extremely hungry; but it was with spirits high that they scanned the panels of each vehicle as it turned into the courtyard. When at last the one appeared bearing the magic inscription "Holyhead to London" on its doors, it was all Mr. Travers could do to prevent himself from rushing forward to meet it. Beside him, Lord Pendril told the terriers they were going to see Miss Helen again, and unrestrained by the conventions they ran up to the door, ears pricked in anticipation. When the steps were let down and only four men descended, the terriers, heads went questionly to one side and they jumped up to investigate the interior. As they snuffled around they discovered traces of the promised scent and barked excitedly, but having checked thoroughly under the seats, they sadly concluded that Helen was no longer there. Whining in puzzlement they returned to Lord Pendril, their short tails tucked pathetically between their legs.

"Well, they were on it, that's plain," his lordship said finally. "Barnaby and Patch don't make mistakes! They weren't on the waybill, so it's ten to one they've had to catch another coach along the road. The point is where?"

Having only traveled in his own carriages, Mr. Travers was not qualified to answer him, but he was not to be thwarted at this stage in his quest. Further inquiries revealed that the Birmingham coach crossed Helen's and Vanessa's route at Stoney Stratford and they hastened to the Swan with Two Necks in London to await it there. But all four passengers had been on for the entire journey and knew nothing of two dark-haired girls.

"We're not going to find them this way," Lord Pendril said, shaking his head. "They could have put up for the night somewhere, or caught the stage, and we can't search every hotel and lodging house in London! Like looking for a needle in a haystack! If you ask me, we'd be better off going to Brighton. For one thing, it's a dashed sight smaller, and for another, it'll be fairly simple to check the coaches as they come in. I vote we stay the night at your place and set off in the morning!"

Mr. Travers agreed this was the most sensible course. Privately he was troubled by the fear that Helen might be gasping for breath somewhere between Daventry and London, and from the unusually serious expression in Lord Pendril's eyes he guessed that his fears were shared. But there was nothing to be gained by voicing them, so they called the terriers away from the wealth of absorbing smells in a corner, rejecting an offer from a man nearby to match them at rat catching against his own two dogs, and climbed once more into the curricle.

Arriving at his house, Mr. Travers cast the staff into a flurry. The downstairs rooms were under covers, the first footman was in his favorite alehouse, and the chef stared despairingly at the raw materials with which he would have to concoct dinner. Indeed, Mr. Travers, after looking around, suggested that they should spend the evening at his club, but uncharacteristically Lord Pendril said he would rather not—he wasn't in the mood for company.

However, by the time they were washed and changed, the efforts of the housekeeper had rendered the place more cheerful. With the covers taken off in the salon, the candles lit, and a fire burning in the grate it appeared welcoming, and Lord Pendril sat

down with a sigh. Barnaby and Patch, similarly tired
by the day, settled in front of the hearth.

At liberty to think ahead calmly, Mr. Travers wondered what would be Vanessa's reaction to his lordship's newfound desire to wed her sister. He remembered her description of the quiet, kind man she had
decided would be a suitable husband for Helen, and
smiled inwardly at the difference between the myth
and the reality. Lord Pendril was certainly kind, and
when he was reminded of his obligations was also
thoughtful, but his wife would need to be tolerant to
a degree. Pondering on the unlikely union, it came to
Mr. Travers that he had never come across a more tolerant woman than Helen and they would probably do
very well together. Lord Pendril's mother might prefer
an alliance with Lady Elizabeth Gnosill, but Helen's
gentle manners would soon win her over and her birth
was perfectly acceptable. His father would be so delighted to discover he at last intended marrying that
Mr. Travers had no doubt he would increase his heir's
allowance to a sum more in keeping with Lord Pendril's notion of bare necessity. How Helen, overcon-
scious of her lameness, would cope with life married to
a social-minded peer was a different matter, but he
suspected that in his lordship's bracing company she
would very soon learn.

With regard to himself and Vanessa he refused to let
his mind picture so far ahead. He had hoped she
loved him and Patty's words seemed to confirm it, but
still he could not completely dismiss the way she had
rejected him. If she would not marry him, in the belief
that he possessed only a modest income, then he
would tell her the truth—he admitted to himself that

he would take her at any price—but it would be a
flaw in their relationship.

If he could find her again.

Neither he nor Lord Pendril mentioned the possibility of failure. After dinner they went early to bed, the
terriers sharing Lord Pendril's couch to the detriment
of the quilt, and at nine o'clock, while Vanessa and
Helen were still at the Swan with Two Necks sleeping
off the effects of their journey, they were on the
Brighton road.

The weather, though still damp, was much better
than the previous day's, and since they were not in the
same haste, they stopped to eat in a civilized manner.
With little discomfort, they arrived on the seafront
halfway through the afternoon, and after surveying
the white-capped waves, once more made inquiries
about two dark-haired young ladies at the inn where
the coach put down. To avoid any possible mistake,
Lord Pendril described Helen's limp with a candor
Mr. Travers at first found startling, but a moment's
reflection convinced him that this was an attitude that
would quickly cure her self-consciousness. The knowledge that Lord Pendril did not attach the slightest importance to it must surely increase her confidence as
nothing else could ever do.

But the ostlers and landlord, after listening to
Lord's description of such lyrical beauties, were able
to say without hesitation that no young ladies like that
had got off, though one ostler volunteered the information that the Mail got in at a quarter after six in the
morning and if they were half as good looking as his
lordship said, he'd be there the following day to
check.

Grinning at the wink that went with his statement,

they went to find Lord Pendril's house. It was situated on the Steyne, and from the outside appeared to be eminently satisfactory. Unfortunately, due to the fact that Lord Pendril was not expected for another week, there was no staff in residence, as they discovered after beating continuously with the knocker.

"Haven't you got a key?" Mr. Travers inquired.

Peering through the window, Lord Pendril said gloomily, "It's at the agent's. I meant to get it on the way here. Let's stay at a hotel!"

"If you think they could be persuaded to take those two animals, by all means!"

Whether it was because hotel proprietors were reluctant to house what were obviously two country-bred ratting dogs, or because, as was stated, they were all full up at the end of June, they were singularly unsuccessful. At the last hotel, the landlord rolled up his eyes and declared that he had not even an attic to spare, which roused Lord Pendril to point out that he hadn't dashed well asked for one.

Outside, Mr. Travers said it might be an idea to get the key to the house before the agent closed for the day. He was more than a little relieved when this was actually in their possession and he was assured that they would at least have a bed to lay their heads on that night, albeit an unmade one, as they discovered on investigating the bedrooms. But peering into various cupboards by the light of a candle they found where the bedlinen was kept and by the simple expedient of laying a sheet on top of the bedclothes then folding them over, made an unsightly but practical cocoon. Regarding his efforts, Mr. Travers said fatalistically that it was not what he was accustomed to but it ⌐uld serve.

They went downstairs again and, leaving a lamp burning in the hall for their return, went out in search of an establishment that would not only cater to the high standards they set on their requirements for dinner, but consent to take in two aggressively hungry terriers. They were more fortunate in this than their pursuit of a room. On the edge of the town they found a small inn that prided itself on its plain but excellent cooking and that boasted a similar dog of its own. Confronted by Barnaby and Patch, the proprietor called on his wife to say if they weren't the very spit of their own Jemmy, who was the best-natured dog in the south. Deplorably, he was later obliged to shut Jemmy up for his own safety since he had such a sunny temperament that he was unable to defend himself. However, even this did not mar the proprietor's goodwill. He said he liked a dog with a bit of spirit and after dinner produced a brandy that had arrived at his back door under cover of darkness, and which Lord Pendril declared was as good as anything in his father's cellars.

Not wishing to spend the rest of the evening in an empty house they lingered over the meal and the brandy, and consequently it was quite late when they walked back. They were further delayed before they could go to bed as neither of them had considered such mundane matters as where the water supply was situated. Having located the pump in the kitchen, Mr. Travers carried a jug of cold water up to his room and found that just as the bed had lacked sheets, so was the room empty of towels. Rather than rummage in cupboards again he dried himself on his shirt and sent up a small prayer of gratitude for the services his position had accustomed him to. It was not until he crawled into his ill-made bed that it occurred to him that not the least of these was that there had always been someone to call him in the morning when he should require it. He went to sleep saying, "I wish to wake at five, I wish to wake at five," but either it was a habit that was only acquired with practice or his hours of driving in the fresh air had induced a heavier sleep than normal. He awoke with a start at six o'clock, it took five minutes to wake Lord Pendril, and not even his best efforts could get them to the inn in time to meet the Mail. It was forty minutes after six when they strode into the courtyard, and the only sign of life was their acquaintance of the previous day.

He grinned when he saw them, and said, "They arrived, and you was right!"

Mr. Travers experienced an indescribable relief. "Where did they go?" he asked urgently.

"That I couldn't tell you, but they hired a carriage and I can find out when the driver gets back!"

"Find the name of the street and the number and there's a guinea in it for you," Mr. Travers promised. "We'll be back again at ten!"

"Why ten?" Lord Pendril inquired as they turned away.

Briefly, Mr. Travers responded, "You haven't seen yourself!"

Rubbing his chin, Lord Pendril said, "Good God! I must look like a sweep! I should frighten the poor girl to death!"

As he viewed himself in the mirror, Mr. Travers realized his own case was no better. Now that he knew Vanessa and Helen were actually in Brighton he was not going to prejudice his chances in any way. There was no kindling to light the kitchen range, so he stripped of his clothes again and carried out an extensive wash in cold water. He then repaired to the nearest hotel to get himself shaved and provided himself with some new neckcloths on the way back to the house, thoughtfully purchasing extra for Lord Pendril, who had been obliged to borrow three from him the night before. After that they returned to the hotel for breakfast, and on Lord Pendril's insistence, collected Barnaby and Patch before once more going back to the inn to discover Helen's and Vanessa's direction.

It was at this juncture that Lord Pendril discovered he was extremely nervous. All his previous amatory adventures had been conducted with the type of woman his mother did not recognize and the idea of forming a closer tie had never entered his head, but it came to him now that he was about to make a proposal of marriage. It was not that he wished to draw back—once Patty had pointed it out he realized that he had every desire to be married and he was convinced he could never love anyone but Helen—it was simply that he did not know how to phrase the request.

He began to drag his feet, but still, all too soon, they were at their destination. The ostler said the coachman couldn't recall the number for sure but he would drive them to the house as he remembered it. He received the guinea for his pains and Mr. Travers and Lord Pendril climbed into the carriage and were taken to a quiet street in an unfashionable part of the town. When the coachman drew up he could not be sure which one it was out of two identical houses, but just as Lord Pendril was blanching at the thought of pulling a stranger's bell at just after ten in the morning, Barnaby and Patch whined excitedly. Noses to the ground they ran up and down outside the railings, and without hesitation dashed up the steps of the house on the right-hand side.

Lord Pendril beamed on them approvingly and Mr. Travers, who had doubted his wisdom in bringing them on such an errand, mounted the steps and gave them a grateful pat. When Lord Pendril had joined him he knocked at the door and stood back.

It seemed an eternity before they heard footsteps, and he had time to recollect that Vanessa had set out at five in the morning and traveled for two days to avoid this meeting. He had no reason to believe her answer would be any different from the one she gave him the first time, and he wondered now if he was a fool or merely besotted.

But on that she opened the door. Mr. Travers, who had taken such pains with his appearance, beheld a pale face with circles under the eyes and untidy hair, and his heart melted.

For a moment she stared at him in disbelief, then her eyes lit up with such unmistakable joy that he knew he had received his final answer. She still stared at him until Barnaby and Patch jumped up to demand a greeting, then she pulled the door back murmuring an apology.

"Mr. Travers! Lord Pendril! You must forgive me. . . . I was not expecting . . . Won't you come in, though I'm afraid we are not settled yet. We only arrived this morning."

Following her, Mr. Travers said, "We know very well what time you arrived, but where did you get to in London?"

"London!" Her eyes flew to his face. "How did you know . . . ?"

"We met the Holyhead Mail, which Barnaby and Patch informed us you had traveled in and we met the Birmingham Mail, which you had never set foot in. By which time we decided we had set ourselves an impossible task and came down to await you here! How is Helen? Did she withstand the traveling?"

"She is perfectly well, though we are both very tired. She is in here." She pushed open the door of the front room as she spoke and the terriers rushed through to wipe their muddy forepaws on the skirt of Helen's gown as they endeavored to jump up to lick her face.

Laughing, she bent down to them and Lord Pendril exclaimed, "Here, I say! Push them off, the dirty little devils!"

She shook her head, smiling. "It doesn't matter! The dress will wash, and oh, I thought I should never see them again!"

With sudden inspiration, he said, "You can have them! Birthday present! I don't know when your birthday is, but it doesn't matter!"

Tears in her eyes, she hugged each of them then stood up. "I could not take them. I love them dearly, but it would not be right. They would be heartbroken at leaving you."

"I thought of a scheme," Lord Pendril said valiantly. "If we got married they wouldn't have to and we could both have them. I'm fond of 'em myself, and I'm fond of you too. In fact I love you! If you don't like the thought you only need say so, but it seemed like a good idea to me."

In the doorway, Mr. Travers pulled Vanessa back into the hall and quietly closed the door.

She smiled at him a little mistily. "I am so glad for

them. Do you know, until last night I had not the smallest inkling that Helen was in love with him. Does that seem absurd to you?"

"Not in the least! Charles didn't realize he was in love with Helen until Patty told him two days ago!" He looked around the dim hallway. "I don't want to seem to criticize, but isn't there anywhere else we could go?"

"Of course!" She flushed slightly. "Come into the parlor at the back. I am afraid it may be a little smoky because I lit a fire and the chimney seems to be damp."

She led the way into a small, cheerless room. Dingy net curtains obscured the light and the view on the garden, and Mr. Travers took a twist of paper and lit the candles in a holder on the shelf. Vanessa looked around with her nose wrinkled in distaste. "You may say what you think! The reality is far removed from the description I was given of it!"

"I imagine it might be," he said drily. "Do you like Brighton?"

"If you mean the town itself, I have hardly had time to find out, but if you are asking if I find my present surroundings congenial, the answer must be obvious! Why do you ask?"

He walked over to the window and parted the curtains to reveal an untended patch of ground and a view of the backs of the houses in the next street. "Because I prefer the country at this season. Charles will want to take Helen to visit his mother, and while she will undoubtedly invite you also, I too have a scheme!"

Watching him she held her breath, and he said, "Will you come back to Priors Cross with me?"

For a long time she was silent, and he repeated, "Will you?"

"Yes." It was hardly more than a whisper and all the animation was wiped from her face.

"To stay with my stepmother," he added.

She raised her eyes quickly to his and he laughed down at her. "You deserve that, Vanessa Hartland, for the manner in which you have played fast and loose with my affections! Now say you will not marry me!"

With a tiny sob, she said, "I thought . . . I did not expect you to ask me again after all those things I said!"

Remorsefully he lifted her chin with his finger. "I'm sorry. That was unworthy of me. Will you, Miss Vanessa Hartland, accept of my hand in marriage?"

She nodded. "If you will believe that I never meant a single word of what I told you!"

He took her in his arms and kissed the top of her head. "In a moment we will discuss who was most to blame—you for telling me what you did or me for believing such nonsense, but in the meantime, may I say that I am certain you are not supposed to cry on an occasion such as this! Look at me!"

Obediently she raised her face and he took out his handkerchief and dried her cheeks. "That's better! Now come and sit down and tell me what it was all about!"

Taking her hand, he led her to the sofa near the smoking fireplace. As they sat down it gushed forth another cloud of smoke and Vanessa chuckled. "What an excessively unromantic setting!"

His arm tightened about her. "Never mind the setting! Why did you try to convince me that your sights were still fixed on this odiously wealthy merchant?"

Gazing at the glimmer of flame that barely managed to survive in the grate, she said, "You are to promise you will not laugh at me!"

"I will promise to try not to," Mr. Travers amended.

Haltingly, she began the story. Put into words it sounded so ridiculous that she could feel her cheeks getting hotter and hotter. Once or twice Mr. Travers's lips twitched, but he did not laugh aloud and her admiration for his forbearance grew. When she came to the end, he smiled down at her. "Vanessa, you are not fit to be let out into the world on your own! Do you realize that I did believe you? If Patty hadn't assured me that it was all nonsense and sent me after you, I should have let you carry out your noble resolve and we should never have seen each other again!"

"I had meant to write to Caroline Harmer," she said hesitantly. "I thought if things altered some day and I had your address . . ."

"A letter addressed to Miss Harmer would never have found her! I too have a confession to make. My motives for what I did, unlike your own, were purely selfish, and you *will* have something to forgive. I have deliberately misled you, on several occasions actually lied to you, and I have involved others in the deception. All I can say in my own justification is that events in the past made it seem reasonable—no, excusable thing to do, and one or two things you said tempted me to continue it. Your letter to Caroline would not have reached her because her name is not Harmer but Travers! She is my sister, or more correctly, my half sister!"

She turned to stare at him, frowning, and he pulled her head on to his shoulder. "Don't look at me like that! Actually, it is all your fault!"

Indignantly, she said, "I should like to know how!"

"I shall prove it to you! To go back to the beginning, my stepmother is an admirable woman with the one fault that she will insist on trying to marry me off. For years she has been inviting what she considers to be suitable girls to my home. Half of them had never set eyes on me before but I think they would have been willing to take me if I had two heads! You see, contrary to what I led you to suppose, my father left me a considerable estate, and most of these young ladies seemed more familiar with the extent of my possessions than I was myself. I began to cherish the dream that one day there would come along a girl, who, to use a hackneyed phrase, would love me for myself alone. And then I met you, and on that first day you announced your intention of wedding a fortune whatever the disadvantages!"

"Oh," Vanessa said in a small voice.

"You see my predicament! The only reason I was staying at the Angel in the first place was because I wished to avoid the latest prospective bride! If I had taken you to the Court, if you had known those bays that so took your fancy were mine, how should I ever have known whether you were influenced by them or not?"

"The Court is *yours?*"

"Yes, my little love!"

Vanessa remembered how impressed she had been by Caroline's casual references to her home and the sense of luxury she had unconsciously conveyed. "Well," she said fair-mindedly, "I'm glad I didn't know before, or I might not have been certain myself! But I do think," she added, with return spirit, "that you might have guessed I did not mean *all* the things I said!"

"My impression was that you most definitely meant them!"

Chuckling, she said, "Well, perhaps I did at the time, but not later!" She was silent for a moment, then she said a trifle nervously, "What will your stepmother think of me after all those other girls? I haven't been presented or . . . or anything, and though my relatives are perfectly respectable, they don't even *know* me!"

Mr. Travers kissed her ear, which was conveniently close. "She already knows I intend marrying you. I met her by chance that day at the fair and she charged me to take you to see her the following day. Frankly, she would love whomever I married. As I said, she is an admirable woman, and the only thing we have ever seriously disagreed on is the fact that she thought it was her duty in life to provide me with a wife. As for your relatives, I suggest that after the wedding we should go on a tour and look them all up."

Vanessa thought of her father's cousin who had shown such a lack of interest in their plight when their mother died, and sighed contentedly at the prospect of arriving at her house behind Mr. Travers's magnificent horses. She was dwelling pleasurably on the vision when the wind gusted in the chimney to send another suffocating cloud forth into the room. Coughing, she went to the window to find it was jammed and flew to open the door while Mr. Travers raked apart the coals in the grate. The timid flame was soon extinguished, but his efforts seemed only to increase the quantity of smoke, and between coughing and laughter she was almost choked.

She went into the hall to lean weakly against the wall, and abandoning the grate, Mr. Travers followed her. The sound of their laughter brought Lord Pendril and Helen out from the other room, and his lordship, peering inquiringly through the haze, demanded to know the source of such a damned pother. He opened the front door to blow it away, and stood on the step for a moment to view the weather.

The rain came down steadily from a solidly gray sky, and calling back the terriers, who had gone out to investigate, he said, "Shocking day! Myself, I don't like Brighton in the wet! Do you girls want to stay on here? I perhaps shouldn't mention it, but it seems a depressing sort of house!"

"It's a *dreadful* house!" Vanessa said, laughing.

His face cleared and he looked across to Mr. Travers. "Well, if they both think so, there's no reason to stay! We can go back up to town and pop the girls in a decent hotel while I make sure m'mother's at home to look after Helen. They can look around the shops! They'll like that. Must make sure Patty arrived safely as well!"

"How . . . ?" Vanessa began, then closed her lips again as it occurred to her that it might not be tactful to inquire in front of her sister how Patty would go on now she had lost her protector.

Mr. Travers regarded her in amusement, correctly divining her thoughts. "Patty is also about to enter into the bonds of matrimony," he told her.

Impulsively, Helen said, "Oh, I am so glad! I did not like to think of . . ."

She broke off in some confusion, but Lord Pendril,

totally unembarrassed, said, "That's right! I forgot to
tell you! Seems she's been thinking about it for some
time, though she never said a word to me! She's a
good girl is Patty!"

"And both Charles and I owe her a great debt of
gratitude," Mr. Travers said gravely. "Without her advice we should still be sitting in the taproom of the
Angel, so I suggest that our first object when we get
to London must be to buy her a superlative wedding
gift!"

Helen and Vanessa nodded agreement, and Lord
Pendril, much struck, exclaimed warmly, "By Jove,
yes!"

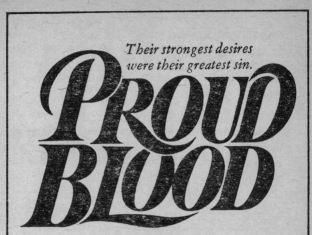

*Their strongest desires
were their greatest sin.*

PROUD BLOOD

by Joy Carroll

She had been born to the golden opulence of
Montreal's ruling class, he to its stormy and
ambitious rival, the French. The dawning of their
passion shocked their Victorian society as a sin
against blood, against pride. Eternally joined,
yet forever divided, they shared a towering love that
survived his faithless hungers and her fiery will—
to blaze unquenched for a lifetime!

A DELL BOOK $1.95

IN 1918 AMERICA FACED AN ENERGY CRISIS

An icy winter gripped the nation. Frozen harbors blocked the movement of coal. Businesses and factories closed. Homes went without heat. Prices skyrocketed. It was America's first energy crisis now long since forgotten, like the winter of '76-'77 and the oil embargo of '73-'74. Unfortunately, forgetting a crisis doesn't solve the problems that cause it. Today, the country is relying too heavily on foreign oil. That reliance is costing us over $40 billion dollars a year. Unless we conserve, the world will soon run out of oil, if we don't run out of money first. So the crises of the past may be forgotten, but the energy problems of today and tomorrow remain to be solved. The best solution is the simplest: conservation. It's something every American can do.

ENERGY CONSERVATION - IT'S YOUR CHANCE TO SAVE, AMERICA

Department of Energy, Washington, D C